High Mountain Stand-Off

His name was Sam Harper and the only sure thing he knew about himself was his skill with a gun. His past was a blank, his future unknown. When he met the beautiful and wealthy Virginia Maitland she was a lone woman desperate for help. With her life under threat from unseen enemies she needed answers.

Together they rode a dangerous trail through the snow-storms, battling the raging elements as well as the men sent out to kill them. And only one thing was written – the crash of gunfire would determine the outcome in a final show-down.

High Mountain Stand-Off

John C. Danner

A Black Horse Western

ROBERT HALE · LONDON

ISBN-10: 0-7090-7991-5
ISBN-13: 978-0-7090-7991-0

Robert Hale Limited
Clerkenwell House
Clerkenwell Green
London EC1R 0HT

Typeset by
Derek Doyle & Associates, Shaw Heath.
Printed and bound in Great Britain by
Antony Rowe Limited, Wiltshire

1

The snowstorm had been raging for two days. Bitter winds, driving down out of Canada had helped to pile up the heavy drifts. Out on the ranges the vast herds of cattle huddled together for warmth and protection from the severe conditions. There was little the ranch crews could do to ease the suffering of the beasts and they were forced to stand back and hope that the majority of cattle would be alive once the storms abated. It was a difficult time for everyone in the territory, even the inhabitants of the settlements. There seemed no let up to the storm and the inhabitants of Butte, Montana Territory, closed their doors and shutters against the hostile elements, resigning themselves to another long night of howling winds and blinding snow. The severe cold had already formed ice on the surface of the banked snow. Thick icicles hung from roof edges, catching the baleful glow of lanterns hung along main street.

There was little movement out of doors. It was the kind of weather only fools or desperate men ventured into. Most of Butte's businesses had closed early due to lack of custom, though a number of the saloons stayed open, likewise a couple of restaurants. Somehow, despite any difficulty, natural or man-made, there was always time for a drink or something to eat.

From the direction of Butte's railroad depot, which was little more than a collection of buildings alongside the tracks, a single figure stumbled defiantly towards the main street. At times completely obscured by the swirling snow, the figure resisted the violent tug of the wind, and after long minutes reached the comparative safety of the closest boardwalk. In the yellow glare of wildly swinging lanterns, the dark shape of the figure took on definite form. A young woman, clad in a thick hooded cloak. The face peering out from behind the fur-lined hood was pale from the cold, yet still showed itself to be beautiful. The shapely mouth was held in a firm, stubborn line and the bright eyes defied the weather to do its worst.

Pulling the wind-whipped cloak closer to her body, Virginia Maitland picked her way along the slippery boardwalk. A few doors along she could see the frosted windows of a restaurant. The glow of lamplight hinted at warmth and comfort inside. She paused for a moment, her hand on the door handle, eyes peering through the misted glass. A gust of wind drove thick swirls of snow at her and she pushed open the door, stumbling inside, a flurry of cold air and whiteness in her wake.

'*Hell's fire*,' a deep male voice yelled. 'Close the damn door.'

Virginia thrust a shoulder against the resisting door and felt it close. She turned away from it, pushing the hood of the cloak back from her face and felt the rush of heat from the room.

'Sorry, ma'am,' the deep voice apologized, 'I didn't realize.'

Virginia glanced at the speaker and saw a stocky, balding man standing at the end of the counter that ran the length of the room. He wore a thick check shirt and a white apron.

'That wind's comin' down off them mountains something fierce,' he went on, still apologetic.

Virginia smiled. 'They said I was foolish leaving the train to come up here,' she said. 'But I saw no reason to just sit there when I could find food.'

'You come from the depot?'

'Yes. It looks as if the train is going to he held up for a long white. They told us the tracks are completely blocked for miles.'

'You hear that, Sam?' the balding man said.

Virginia glanced around and became aware of the restaurant's occupants. There were only six tables in the room. Three of them were in use. A middle-aged man was seated at the table closest to the door. At another were three hard-faced men wearing thick coats and heavy boots. One of them had a rifle leaning against the table close to his left hand. All three of the men had turned to stare at Virginia. There was something in their gaze that unsettled her and she looked away, toward the last of the occupied tables. It was in the furthest corner of the restaurant, facing the door. The single occupant had his chair wedged into the very corner of the wall. He sat slumped in the chair, his body hunched up in the thick, hip-length coat he was wearing. His wide-brimmed hat was drawn down across his face, shadow falling across his jaw. The remains of a meal were on the table in front of him; he looked as

7

if he was asleep.

'I hear,' the middle-aged man grumbled.

'Don't appear you'll be getting back to Anaconda for a while.'

The man named Sam picked up his cup and swilled the coffee round. 'You better brew me up some more of your awful coffee then, Bernie. Looks like I'm going to need it.'

'Bide your time,' Bernie said. 'Let me attend to the lady first. Ma'am, if you'd like to find yourself a table.'

Virginia nodded and crossed the room. She had noticed the pot belly stove at the far end of the restaurant. There was an empty table close by. Ignoring the open stares of the trio still watching her, she crossed to the table and sat down, feeling the heat from the stove. It felt good. Far better than the chill of the cold carriage she had left behind. She hoped there was a hotel in town. A comfortable bed was what she would be needing after a hot meal. She leaned back in the chair, the warmth from the stove relaxing her. She took off her gloves. Brushed stray locks of her soft, dark hair from her face.

'*Ma'am?*'

Virginia glanced up. It was the man called Bernie.

'Could I have some coffee? And something to eat, please.'

'Sure. Now I don't have anything too fancy, ma'am. There's some beef stew. Or a steak. Potatoes and greens.'

'The stew, I think,' Virginia said. 'By the way, is there a hotel in town?'

'Yes, ma'am. We got a couple. Ain't palaces but they do.'

Virginia nodded. Bernie went away, leaving her to enjoy the warmth from the stove. It made her drowsy. Virginia knew it was more than just the heat. She was tired. Despite the need to continue her journey, she knew that what she really needed was a chance to rest. Too many days had passed, most of them a blur in her memory, and she was fast becoming aware of her physical condition. As she had done many times previously, she asked herself the same question – *had she been too impulsive taking on the responsibility of this journey? Had she been wrong in her decision not to let anyone know what she intended?* And as before she told herself she had done the right thing. The situation in which she found herself had put her in the position of not knowing who to trust. The thought saddened her, but only strengthened her resolve. No matter what she had to face she would go on. She had come too far to give up now, and it was not in her nature to back away from her problems.

'Coffee, ma'am?'

The words snapped her out of her lethargic state with a jerk. For a moment Virginia stared at the face of the restaurant owner, then her jangled senses sorted themselves out and she gave an embarrassed smile.

'I hope I can stay awake long enough to do justice to your food,' she said, by way of an apology.

'I'll hurry it along, ma'am,' he said, placing the mug in front of her.

Virginia sipped the hot coffee. There was little sound inside the restaurant and she could hear the droning howl of the wind. Glancing towards the window she saw the white swirl of the falling snow.

Her meal arrived a little time later. She found herself pleasantly surprised. Not only was it well cooked, it also tasted good. Despite her weariness she found herself tuck-

9

ing into the meal with a renewed appetite. While she was eating the three men who had been sharing a table got up and left the restaurant. As the last man went out through the door a muffled figure pushed by him, stepping just inside. Virginia glanced up at the blast of cold air that gusted across the room. She found herself looking into the face of the newcomer and felt a moment of sudden alarm. There was something about the way he was staring at her, his hard, angry eyes taking in every detail. For a moment, the angular, hollow-cheeked face turned in Victoria's direction, and it was almost as if he had found what he was looking for. He turned and left, closing the door with a bang, leaving only a white streak of snow on the floor.

'Now who was that?' Bernie asked.

The man, Sam, shrugged. 'Damned if I know,' he said, then added, 'Tell you one thing. He looked mean enough to cut your throat for a silver dollar. Beggin' your pardon, ma'am,' he said for Victoria's benefit.

'I think you could be right,' she agreed.

The matter was not mentioned again, but Victoria found herself imagining the man's face over and over in her mind. She couldn't help but wonder who he was, and why he had been staring around the restaurant so intently. She wondered if she was simply over-reacting. The man could have been looking for a friend. Then just as easily he might have been looking for *her*. It was possible that despite all her precautions, her journey and destination could have been discovered. If that had happened then she might easily find herself in trouble.

She finished her meal and paid her bill. Pausing beside the stove for a final warm Virginia drew the hood of her cloak over her head and pulled on her gloves.

Bernie had been watching her quietly. 'You sure you'll be all right out there, ma'am?'

'Yes. I made it from the train so I should manage a few more yards to the hotel, thank you.'

Once outside, the door closing off the comfort and warmth of the restaurant, she felt the full force of the storm. The wind seemed stronger and the snow heavier. Virginia kept close to the store fronts as she made her uneasy way along the boardwalk. It was hard to see for more than a few yards ahead. After that everything vanished in a white, swirling mist. Virginia felt as if she was the only person on the street. She might have been the only person in town. Butte seemed devoid of life.

Looking up and down the street she saw no one. There was just the swirling snow, eddying back and forth, occasional gusting aside to reveal a soft glow of lamplight behind window glass. Smoke from chimneys was scattered the moment it emerged, but it did remind Virginia that inside those buildings people were huddled around their glowing stoves, at least warm and comfortable, while she was foolishly exposing herself to the elements.

As if in contradiction to her thoughts, a dark figure appeared in front of her. Virginia gasped, surprised by the sudden appearance. Shielding her eyes with a gloved hand she peered up into the face of the figure. The pale light from a wildly swinging lantern illuminated the man's gaunt features, and Virginia recognized the man who had appeared in the restaurant.

'*What do you want?*' she asked, a rising anger replacing her original fright.

The man's response was to grin at her. It made him look

even more menacing. He lunged forward, his arms rising from his sides, long-fingered hands reaching for her. Virginia stepped back, turning to avoid his grasp. But the fingers of one hand hooked in the folds of her cloak and she felt herself being dragged back. Her feet slipped on the thick snow and she stumbled. She heard the man grunt. Twisting her face towards him she caught a blurred glimpse of his body bending over her.

'*You'll come with me if I have to carry you!*' His words were torn away by the wind almost as he uttered them, but Virginia understood their meaning. It made her realize that her fears had not been groundless: her journey here *had* been discovered.

Strong fingers gripped her arm. She was yanked savagely to her feet. Virginia responded without thinking. Her left hand lashed out, catching the man across the bridge of his nose. The blow stung and he swore. And then he hit her back, his palm slapping across her exposed cheek. Virginia fell back against the door post of a dark, shuttered store. The pain of the slap only increased her stubbornness. She kicked out with the toe of her high leather boot catching the man just below the knee. He let go of her, falling back a step, a string of curses flowing from his lips.

Virginia turned to go by him, hoping for at least a chance of escape. But again was denied the chance. The man took a couple of long strides, his hands catching and gripping her body. Virginia fought him silently, quickly realizing that his strength was too much for her. Despite that she found that she wasn't afraid of him. Probably because there was little time to do anything but put up as much resistance as she could.

And then the fingers cruelly digging into her flesh slid away. She heard the man groan, a pained sound. She lifted her head in time to see her attacker stumble away from her. His face, gleaming in the light of a lantern, was twisted in agony.

Another figure stepped into view, moving towards Virginia's attacker. There was a flurry of subdued sound. Something metallic shone in the light. Virginia heard a solid thumping sound and a dark figure hunched to the boardwalk.

Silence fell again. It seemed to blot out everything for a moment. Then Virginia became aware of her own harsh breathing. Now she could feel herself trembling. As her awareness returned, she realized how cold she was. She could feel the bitter slap of the wind against her face.

'Can you stay on your feet?'

Virginia glanced at the speaker. She found something familiar in him, and after a few seconds she recognized him as the man from the restaurant: the silent figure sitting in a corner of the room, the remains of a meal on the table in front of him. Even now she could not see his face; only the merest reflection of light in his dark eyes.

'I'll manage,' she told him bluntly. The fact that he'd just come to her assistance didn't give him the right to speak to her with such brusqueness, she decided.

'Hotel's just along here.'

Virginia felt his big hand grip her arm. There was strength in the hand, she could feel it, but it was controlled. She found herself being escorted along the slippery boardwalk, and she knew there was no sense in arguing with this man – whoever he was.

'Lookin' at you a man might think you had sense. Then

you go and do a damn fool thing like this!'

Trembling with anger, Virginia tore herself from his grasp. She braced herself against the force of the wind, turning to face her rescuer.

'Just what did I do that makes you so arrogantly superior?'

'When that feller showed his face back in the restaurant you knew he was looking for you. I was sitting in back of you and there was no way of missing how you nearly jumped off your chair. He made you sit up and take notice. And then you get up and walk outside just the way he'd hoped you would.'

Virginia opened her mouth to reply. But she remained silent. She knew that she had been foolish. *Though what else could she have done?* She was alone in what she was facing. Or she had been until this strange and violent man had stepped into her life.

'Come on,' he said grudgingly, taking her arm again and almost dragging her along the boardwalk.

They reached the hotel. Virginia felt herself being propelled through the opened door and into the dimly lit, stuffy lobby. She took a moment to regain her breath, shaking the snow from her clothing. Behind her the door closed, cutting off the howl of the wind. The tall figure of the man strode past her and up to the reception desk.

'Hey, Milton, get out here.'

A skinny youth appeared. He was pale and pimply and wore huge, steel-rimmed spectacles. His straggly hair kept falling forward across his eyes and he blinked constantly. He wore multi-coloured suspenders over his rumpled shirt, half of which hung out of his pants.

'Lady here needs a room, Milton,' the man said. 'She's

off the train stuck down at the depot. Better give her number eight.'

Milton nodded. He opened the thick register on the desk in front of him, pushing it in Virginia's direction. He turned the big book around and indicated a line for her to sign on with a grimy finger. 'You sign here, ma'am.'

Virginia took the pen he handed her. As she filled in the required information she could feel Milton's eyes on her. When she glanced up he looked away quickly.

'My luggage is still at the depot,' Virginia said.

'Milton can arrange to have it brought up. Can't you, Milton?'

Milton almost said no but he changed his mind when he caught the man's expression.

'Sure,' he said hastily. He took a tagged key from the board behind him and gave it to Virginia.

Virginia let herself be escorted upstairs and along the narrow, shadowed corridor. Outside room eight she paused, turning to face the silent figure beside her.

'Just why did you choose number eight?' she asked.

'It's next door to mine,' he said simply, as if that explained everything.

Virginia smiled wryly. 'Oh! Do you think I'll be needing your help again?'

'I wouldn't be at all surprised.'

He turned to go. Almost without realizing what she was doing, Virginia reached out to touch his arm. He turned back towards her, his head lifting, and for the first time Virginia was able to see his face dearly. Beneath the dark stubble and without the near-scowl it could have passed for handsome, though there was no softness to it at the moment. No trace of weakness. Even the eyes mirrored the exterior hardness. Virginia felt a faint shiver run through her. She couldn't explain why. This man didn't frighten her, but she realized that she had become aware of his potential violence. He was not a man to be trifled with. Now she recalled the way the desk clerk had behaved and she could see why. This man had no need to advertise himself. People only needed to look at him, talk to him, to know who and what they were dealing with. The thought ran through Virginia's mind that this was the kind of man she could do with at her side.

Perhaps. . . .

She realized her hand was still touching his arm. She drew back slowly.

'I just wanted to say thank you for what you did. Mister. . . ?'

A humourless smile ghosted across his stern mouth before he spoke, forming the word as if he wasn't sure of it himself.

'Name's Harper, ma'am.'

Not giving Virginia time to respond, he turned and walked to the door of his own room. Without a backward glance he opened the door and stepped inside, closing the door firmly after him. He left Virginia Maitland staring after him, angry and intrigued at the same time, and also confused as to why he was having such an effect on her. She was still trying to puzzle it out as she entered her own room, securely locking her door before she crossed over to the bed. . . .

2

Struggling out of the thick coat Sam Harper tossed it across the foot of the bed. He flung his hat on top of the coat. He stood for a moment in the middle of the room, staring moodily at the thick snow swirling outside his window. Not for the first time did he declare himself a damn fool for coming to such a Godforsaken place as Butte in the middle of what looked like the worst winter in history. Not that he'd had any other place to go. All he'd wanted was to get out of San Felipe and the fussy ministrations of that damn doctor. Three weeks he'd been in that place. He'd been just about ready to crawl up the wall by then – but if he'd been thinking he'd had enough there was more to come. The doc, the local marshal, they wouldn't leave him alone. Dogging him from morning till night. Questions and more questions. He'd taken it until he could take no more. After that he just let go at them. He'd never believed a room could empty of people so quickly. After that it was only the doctor who came to see him. Harper figured he could do with that but only up to a point. He had enough to handle on his own, because he knew nothing of himself apart from his name – and only that because someone had told him what it was.

When the stern-faced doctor had explained what was wrong with him, Harper's first reaction had been stunned silence. It took a little swallowing. The silence had helped to conceal a fair amount of initial panic. He'd figured he had a right to be scared. It wasn't every day a man lost his identity, his past, and found himself mentally naked. He had no knowledge of his former character, how he might have acted in such a situation, and it left him off-guard, somehow unable to cope. But a little while later, left alone, he had been able to rationalize his feelings. Get himself sorted out. There was no point in fretting over what had happened. He had to accept it and make the best of it. Acceptance, however, didn't help too much. And, as the time slid by and he got stronger he began to get restless. He found himself wondering if that was part of his old self. Had he been the restless kind? Unable to put up with inactivity? Wanting some kind of distraction? He had some luck in that direction when he was allowed to leave the hospital after a couple more days. The bullet wounds he'd received, including the one that had gouged his scalp, were healing well. All he needed was rest. Time would do the repairs. He'd asked how *much* time – but the doctor couldn't tell him. Whatever healing process there was, it lay inside his head, and the body had its own timetable for recovery. It might take a month, six months, a year! It might never right itself. The doctor's last statement was ringing in his ears, and he felt like a new born baby tossed out onto the street. Something would slip into the conscious stream of his thoughts, just long enough for Harper to become aware, but then it would drift away before he could grasp it, leaving him coldly fuming at his inability to take command of his own memory. He found he had a grey, shifting mass of imagery on the fringe of his conscious mind. Partly composed pictures of faces, of places, names which refused to reach his lips. Yet even this help did little to satisfy Harper.

The long days drifted by in a haze. Harper stared at the walls of his room in the hotel in San Felipe until he could take no more. In the early hours of a chilly morning he got dressed. He strapped on the gunbelt and dropped the big Colt into the holster. The gun had been with him during his time in the hotel room. It was the only thing he had any union with. The weapon felt familiar to him, and he didn't need telling that the Colt was an important part of his life. He had no way of knowing why. He just knew it was a link with his past. His only one, and he had no intention of losing it. With his saddle-bags over his shoulder, Harper had slipped quietly out of the hotel. He'd been told he had a horse at the livery but he had decided against riding out. His condition had left him weak, so he figured taking the train might be less of a strain and would at least give him time to rest up. He made his way to the depot and bought himself a ticket on the first train out, and when that one reached the end of the line he picked up another. He travelled in this haphazard fashion for over a week. He had no destination, no final resting place. Just a need to be on the move. To be alone. Away from the claustrophobic atmosphere of San Felipe where there were too many people asking too many questions. He found that he felt more at ease out on the vast, sprawling open countryside. A small part of his character began to show itself. He was in harmony with this wild land. He felt it deep inside.

Despite his yearning to travel he finally tired of the long, boring days sitting in draughty carriages, staring out

19

at emptiness, with only the mournful sound of the train whistle breaking the silence of the wilderness. On a bitterly cold afternoon, Harper had stepped down from the train that had brought him to the snow-covered township of Butte in the Montana Territory. At the back of his mind was a vague feeling that told him he'd been here before. Perhaps some memory had drawn him back again. He couldn't be sure, and he didn't feel that it mattered. Tramping up into town through the crisp, frozen snow, Harper had picked out a hotel, booked a room, and had settled in for an indefinite stay. He had enough money to see him through the winter, and if nobody found him he figured he could find satisfaction here.

A couple of weeks later, with Butte practically cut off, Harper had begun to question his choice of refuge. He had sampled Butte's complete range of amenities, and he was beginning to feel as if he was back in San Felipe. He was bored, impatient with his mind's refusal to return to its normal condition, and he desperately needed some kind of distraction. That had been the night a beautiful young woman named Virginia Maitland had stepped into his life. Harper had involved himself in her affairs without an invitation, knowing exactly what he was doing, and somehow accepting the fact that he was bound to regret his actions sometime in the not too distant future. . . .

Harper turned away from the window. He stretched out on his bed and gazed up at the ceiling, following a long, zigzag crack that ran from one corner to the other. He thought about Virginia Maitland, trying to figure out what *she* was doing in a Godforsaken place like Butte in the middle of winter. He had thoughts, too, about the man who had attacked her. The man had been something more than just an over-excited drunk after a bit of company. He'd deliberately waited for the woman, biding his time in the darkness, and if Harper's curiosity hadn't been aroused he would have got away with whatever he'd intended. Virginia Maitland was evidently a young woman in demand for some reason. Harper wished he knew what. That would have to come later.

He dragged the blankets over him, deciding to sleep on the matter. He found sleep hard because he couldn't get it out of his mind that Virginia Maitland was in the next room, and he realized now that that was just a little too close for comfort. His comfort!

His next clear recollection was of someone rapping sharply on the door of his room. Harper sat up, tossing the blankets off his legs. He lurched off the bed, rubbing a hand across his stiff face. Still half asleep he located the door and yanked it open.

'Good morning, Mr Harper.'

Harper stared into Virginia Maitland's smiling face and tried to understand the logic behind anyone being so damn cheerful so early in the day. He glanced over his shoulder. Beyond the window of his room snow was still falling heavily out of a lead-grey sky.

'What time is it?' he asked.

Virginia laughed softly. 'Almost seven-thirty,' she said.

'God, woman, what're you thinking of!' Harper turned away from her in disgust. He crossed to the washstand and picked up the big jug, spilling water into the basin. His flesh cringed when he splashed the icy liquid over his face. He snatched up the towel and dried his face.

'I would like you to be my guest for breakfast, Mr Harper,' he heard Virginia say.

'It's about the best offer I've had today.' Harper peered at his face in the mirror and decided he could get away without a shave. He ran a comb through his dark hair. 'You mind if I put on a fresh shirt first?' he asked.

'Shall I leave?' Virginia asked, not entirely hiding the amusement in her tone.

'I figure you're old enough to make up your own mind about that.'

She stepped into the room and closed the door.

'Have you come to Butte for any particular reason, Mr Harper?' she asked pointedly.

Harper looked up from unfolding a clean shirt. 'Happened to be where the train stopped.' He stripped off his creased shirt and tossed it on the bed. 'Isn't too polite to ask too many questions like that.'

'I had my reasons,' she said. Her eyes were drawn to the scars and the puckered tissue of old wounds marking his hard-muscled torso. Almost guiltily, she looked into his face. 'I need to know whether or not you have a job, Mr Harper, because if the answer is no I can offer you employment. If you think you might be interested.'

Harper picked up his coat and hat. 'Let's go,' he said. 'I talk a whole lot better on a full stomach.'

3

'More coffee, Mr Harper?'

Harper nodded and pushed his cup across the table. He watched as Virginia filled it, appreciating the opportunity of being able to take a good look at her. It only confirmed an earlier opinion – she was a beautiful young woman. He had no doubts on that score.

'Do I pass your inspection, Mr Harper?' Virginia asked, her eyes lifting from the filled coffee cup.

'Bernie cooks a good breakfast,' Harper said casually. 'Don't you think so?'

Virginia smiled. 'Yes, Mr Harper, he does.'

They were the only customers at this early hour. Harper had chosen the same table he'd been using the previous evening. They had eaten their meal in comparative silence. Despite her earlier mood of calm, Virginia had begun to show signs of unease.

'I think it's time I offered you an explanation, Mr Harper,' Virginia said. She paused for a moment, searching for the right words, which she had been putting together all through the meal. Now, though, none of them seemed to fit. 'You have probably realized by my accent that I am English. My home is a small village in Buckinghamshire, not far from London. For the past few years, however, I have spent a great deal of time in America. Until nine months ago I accompanied my father on his business trips. He became ill very suddenly and died within a week. I was left an inheritance comprising of a large number of businesses, both here and in England. My mother died many years ago and I have no brothers or sisters. My father, thankfully, was a man who did not allow discrimination to get in the way of ability. The fact that I was a woman made no difference to my being taught all about his considerable business enterprises. And I enjoyed the opportunity. To be honest, Mr Harper, I was surprised when my father's will became known. He had left everything to me. His entire business empire and his money. Financially I am an extremely wealthy woman. If I closed down all the businesses tomorrow I would still have more than enough money to live on. In hard cash alone I am worth somewhere in the region of four million dollars. I am telling you this to show you that I am not just an empty-headed woman acting on impulse. I pride myself on being capable of rational decisions.'

'Was it a rational decision that brought you out here in the middle of winter?'

'The situation, Mr Harper, demanded that I act without delay. It is unfortunate that we cannot always control every aspect of every situation that occurs. However, I do not intend to let a snowstorm stop me.'

He toyed with his cup of coffee. 'What about *aspects* like that feller last night? Appeared to me you were having difficulty controlling him.'

Virginia glared at him but resisted the urge to argue. 'I don't deny the fact I was in trouble before you came along. Which is why I have a proposition to put to you. If you are interested.'

'Go on.'

'Before I come to that I'd like to explain why I am here. North of Butte, about two days' ride, is a town called Bannock, the centre of an area supporting a number of copper mines. Three of the mines belong to me. My father was one of the first to start mining around Bannock. The largest of the mines – *Maitland One* – has the highest yield of copper ore for miles around. It has one of the richest veins ever discovered. To date it has been producing for nearly three years and shows no sign of running out.'

'So what's your problem?'

'My father always believed in paying good wages, looking after the men who worked for him. The mines at Bannock are no exception. Despite that fact there has been a considerable amount of trouble. More than once production has been disrupted. Men have been attacked. Company property has been destroyed. Three times, wagons taking ore to the smelter at Anaconda have been stolen. A man died during one of the thefts. A man who worked for me.'

'What about the local law?' Harper. asked.

Virginia smiled. 'Perhaps you haven't had much to do with mining towns, Mr Harper. If you had you would know that they are their own law. They make their own rules and expect everyone to abide by those rules. A town like Bannock is a closed community. It lives for the mines, and the mines need the town. Each is a part of the other.

Bannock looks after its own. Nobody interferes with a town like Bannock. Copper is an extremely valuable commodity, Mr Harper. Not only is it used in this country, it is also exported. As far as Washington is concerned, they are happy to leave places like Bannock alone as long as the ore keeps coming out. Short of mass-murder and civil war the outside world will leave Bannock to deal with its own problems.'

'Sounds the kind of situation just ripe for trouble.'

'I think that is what's happened in Bannock. I've based my suspicions on a number of letters received from the man responsible for managing the three Maitland mines. His name is Jack Bell. I know him personally. He has worked for my father for many years. He knows his job and he knows mining towns. And the facts he put in the letters he sent to me all point to the same thing: that there is trouble. He talks of frightened miners. Of hired thugs terrorizing them. Accidents. Thefts. His last letter was the one which prompted me to come here. In it he said that he had found out what was going on but he was sure that the people responsible were on to him. I think he's in trouble, Mr Harper. For his sake and for the men who work in those mines I have to get to Bannock to find out what is happening.'

Harper shook his head slowly. 'Damnit, couldn't you have sent someone else?'

'*Who?* Jack Bell said in one of his letters that he had got to the point where he trusted no one. Not even his own administration staff. He felt sure that someone amongst his own staff was working for the people responsible for the troubles. It made me realize that there might be someone in my own organization doing exactly the same. How could I confide in anyone? Which face could I trust? My father had always believed in going out and dealing with the dirty jobs himself. So I decided to do the same. I know my way around mining camps and I also know the business. If there's something going on I'll find out what it is. The only problem is that it seems my presence has already become common knowledge. I told no one in New York where I was going, or what I intended doing. But someone did find out and warned Bannock. The proof came in the shape of that man last night.'

'Where I came in,' Harper remarked.

Virginia nodded. 'And where I'd like you to stay,' she said. 'Mr Harper, determination and logic are all right in their place, but I'm no good against violent men or the threat of physical harm. I know this and that is why I would like to hire you to guide me to Bannock, and to stay by my side all the time, wherever I go.'

'That could be both interesting and downright embarrassing.'

'And that would be *all the time* with reservations, Mr Harper.'

'You could be walking in on a hell of lot more trouble than you ever dreamed of. If these people do exist, and they've realized you might be on to them, they might decide to stop you the *permanent* way.'

'The thought had crossed my mind, Mr Harper. But you carry a gun, don't you?

'Yes.'

'And you know how to use it, I presume?'

'Dare say I do.'

Virginia smiled. 'Then I think we have covered all the

relevant points. Except the matter of your fee, of course.'

'Depends on whether I take the job,' Harper said.

Virginia nodded. 'Obviously. Do you need time to consider my offer?'

'No,' he told her. 'I'll take it.'

'Thank you, Mr Harper.'

'Couple of things we'd better organize first,' Harper said. 'We're going to need a couple of good horses. Food, blankets and the like.'

Virginia opened the leather drawstring bag she carried. She took out a thick roll of banknotes and peeled off a number. She placed them on the table in front of Harper.

'I'll leave it to you, Mr Harper, to purchase whatever we need to get us to Bannock. If you need more just let me know.' She glanced at the roll of notes in her hand. 'Now about your fee. . . .'

'We can talk about that later. I ain't going to have much need for money between here and Bannock.' Harper picked up the money Virginia had placed in front of him. 'You go back to the hotel and wait for me there.'

He stood up and made for the door, fastening the collar of his coat.

Stepping outside he caught the cold slap of the snow-laden wind across his face. Tugging his hat brim lower he plunged through the deep snow covering the street. There was a good livery stable at the far end of Butte's meandering street. The owner was a taciturn, rawboned man named Abel Hirsch. Harper had rented a horse from him once, and he knew that Hirsch was a good man with horseflesh. He found the man already in his cramped office just inside the livery's wide doors, hunched over as he drew warmth from the glowing pot-bellied stove. Hirsch barely glanced up as Harper pushed into the office, stretching out his hands towards the stove.

'Good day for business,' Harper said.

Hirsch only grunted, not even looking up from the paperwork he was doing. The tiny office was silent except for the brittle scratching of Hirsch's pen across paper as he returned to his work.

'You want to do this deal or not?' Harper asked.

Hirsch glanced over his shoulder. '*What deal?*' he wanted to know.

'I want to buy a couple of good, strong horses, complete with saddles and trappings. No crow bait. I need animals that can stand up on their own. I ain't bothered about speed but I am bothered about staying power.'

'What you planning on? Going mountain climbing?'

Harper grinned. 'You could be right there.'

Twenty minutes later, Harper left the livery. He had bought a pair of good horses, saddles and trappings. His next stop was a store he knew. There he would be able to get the supplies he and Virginia were going to need.

The livery faded into the white swirl of snow behind him. Harper cut across an open stretch of ground lying between the livery and the first of Butte's business premises. His hands were thrust deeply into the pockets of his coat, his head lowered against the driving wind and snow. As he neared the first of the buildings he heard the too-familiar, flat sound of a pistol shot. He let his knees go, dropping to the hard ground, while his right hand jerked the heavy Colt from his holster. He hit the ground, twisting his body round in the direction of the shot. As his head came around he saw a wink of flame and then heard the same sound as before. This bullet was closer. It mush-roomed into the ground, peppering his face with slivers of stone. Harper swore. He levelled his Colt, aimed and loosed off two fast shots. Following on the second shot came the sound of a man yelling in pain. Harper kicked to his feet and ran along the side of the building, looking for his attacker. He rounded the end of the building as a gun blasted. The bullet bit deeply into the thick corner post, chewing a large sliver of wood from the post. As he straightened up from his involuntary ducking movement, Harper caught sight of a dark figure racing away from him. He lunged forward, his anger spurring him on. The distant figure appeared to be limping, and Harper wondered if it was because of one of his shots; he remem-bered the sudden cry of pain. He saw the snow-blurred figure hesitate. Harper blinked his eyes against the snow, then he heard the gun fire. He felt something tug his left sleeve and gave a grunt of annoyance as a hot pain streaked across his arm. He dropped to his knees in the wet snow, lifting his Colt, using his left hand as extra support as he levelled the gun. The Colt's black muzzle flickered twice with flame. Thick, acrid powder smoke curled into the air. Before the smoke obscured his vision, Harper saw the dark figure fall back as if struck by a power-ful force.

Harper climbed to his feet. He felt drained, all the excitement of the past seconds wiped away. Suddenly he felt cold. His left arm was beginning to ache. He trudged slowly through the snow towards the place he'd seen the dark figure fall. He found he was holding the big Colt tightly in his fist, and for no apparent reason he wondered if this was always how it was. Did he always feel like this after he'd killed a man? He stopped walking. The flickering shadows of the past rose briefly in his mind, taunting him with grey images, still too indistinct for him to grasp. But a fragment had slipped through. He knew now that this was not the first gunfight he'd been involved in. And he was aware, too, that he had reacted instinctively to the first shot. His body had taken over and he had gone through the motions without hesitation. It was only a tiny part of his real self, but it was a beginning. He had learned little about his past life in San Felipe, and this revelation made him wonder why. Was it because his past was best forgotten? A lesser man might have shrugged the thought aside. Sam Harper found he could not. The less he knew about his former existence, no matter how sordid it might turn out to be, only made him more determined to expose it all.

Snow was already starting to cover the body. Harper crouched beside it. He knew before he touched the man that he was dead, and when he saw the bloody hole in the chest and the other one through the throat there was no point in checking further. He spotted, too, the blood-stained trouser leg. His first hit. Harper flicked snow from the dead face. He recognized the man who had come into the restaurant. The same one who had attacked Virginia outside a short time later. *Why had he tried to kill Harper?* Because he had involved himself in Virginia's problems? Or had it been just a personal vendetta? Revenge for something Harper had done to him in the past? Harper stood up. Whatever the reason, it had died with the man.

He turned away and headed back for the street. In a while the body would be hidden by the falling snow. The

31

way it was coming down it might be spring before the body was found. Harper didn't want problems now. He wanted to get Virginia Maitland away from Butte as quickly as possible. The last thing he wanted was to have to answer a lot of questions. He reached the street and paused, glancing in both directions. The town still looked as if it was completely deserted. The gunshots seemed to have gone unnoticed. Probably snatched away by the wind before anyone heard them. Harper realized he was still holding his own gun. He shoved it back in the holster and made his way towards the store he'd been planning to visit before the appearance of the man he'd had to kill.

Inside the cluttered store, Harper told the man behind the counter what he wanted. The owner eyed him suspiciously at first, his steady gaze soon coming to rest on the long tear in the sleeve of Harpers coat which was moist with blood. His interest in it was soon dissipated by the production of Harper's money. The storekeeper's eyes lit up at the thought of a substantial cash transaction and he clucked his sympathy at Harper's casual mention of the *damn rusty nail* he'd caught his coat on down at the livery. By the time Harper left the store the owner was busy adding up his profit, the blood-stained sleeve forgotten.

Harper made his way back to the hotel. He carried a wrapped parcel under one arm. The bulk of his purchase was still in the store. They would pick it up on the way out of Butte.

He went straight upstairs and knocked on Virginia's door.

'I want to talk,' he said as she opened her door. 'My room.'

Virginia nodded and followed him to his room. Letting her step by him, Harper closed the door. He tossed the parcel onto his bed.

'Brought you some clothes,' he said.

'But I have clothing,' Virginia protested.

'Not for where we're going,' Harper told her. 'Weather like this you don't get a second chance if you make a mistake.'

Virginia picked up the parcel. 'Whatever you say, Mr Harper.' She watched him open his coat and slip it off, and then she spotted the wet bloodstain on his shirtsleeve. 'Good heavens, what happened?'

Harper took off his shirt and inspected the ragged furrow in his arm. 'Your friend from last night. He must have taken offence at me laying my gun barrel across his head. He was waiting for me out near the livery. If he'd been a better shot you'd be on the lookout for another guide.'

A look of horror crossed Virginia's face. 'Are you trying to say he meant to kill you?'

'When a man comes at you with a gun, and he's using that gun, it's a sure bet he ain't makin' collections for the church fund.'

'What have I got you into, Mr Harper?' Virginia's tone revealed her genuine shock.

'Miss Maitland, it appears it ain't the first time I been shot at. An' likely it ain't about to be the last time I'll have to shoot a man. So don't you worry over it.'

It took him a moment to realize what he had just said. Without conscious thought he had stated the fact being shot at was no first-time occurrence. Something he had remembered from his past? A knowledge once hidden in the recesses of his blanked out mind rising to the surface? *Was this how it would be?* Small fragments coming into the light from the dark mire of memory loss? He didn't dwell on it. Better to let it return of its own accord.

Virginia had crossed to the washstand to pour water into the basin. Now she brought it across to the bed and set the bowl down on the chair standing against the wall. She soaked a corner of a towel in the water, turned to Harper, and began to clean the shallow wound.

'You say you shot him?'

'Yeah.' Harper turned his head a little. Just enough so that he could smell the faint perfume she was wearing.

'Is he hurt badly?'

'He's dead,' Harper said evenly. He heard her gasp and felt her hand falter. 'He was set on killing *me*, an' I'm not ready to die yet. Not in some back alley and especially not for the reason he was doing it.'

'What do we do now, Mr Harper?'

'Just what we already decided to do. Collect the horses I bought. Pick up our supplies, and start for Bannock.'

'But what about that man? What will happen when his body is found?'

Harper pulled his remaining clean shirt from his saddle-bag, and slipped it on, glad now that he'd added a couple of new ones to the list he'd gone through at the store.

'In another hour that feller will be lying at the bottom of a snowdrift. Nobody's going to find him until it thaws and that won't be for a damn long time. I ain't about to sit around waitin' to see if he's got any friends hanging around. No way of knowing if he went after me because I put him down last night, or because I got myself involved with you. Either way it can only mean trouble if we hang around Butte. So we'll move. That feller ain't about to go anywhere. He'll he there come spring and by then we'll likely be able to explain the why and the what about the way he died.'

Virginia picked up the parcel of clothing. At the door she said, 'I'm sorry it had to happen, Mr Harper, but I'm glad you weren't hurt badly.'

'I'll drink to that! Now go and get ready. I want to move as soon as possible.'

Before he did anything else Harper reloaded his Colt. Sitting on the edge of the bed, thumbing fresh bullets into the chambers, he ran over the morning's events. It was strange, he thought. A day ago he had been fretting over the lack of action in Butte. Now he was anxious to leave the town because of the threat of more. Not that he was afraid of the physical involvement, but because here in Butte he was at a disadvantage. A town could hide strange faces from him. Out in the open country a man could spot his enemies at a distance, and plan accordingly. He could decide on his own ground and fight from there. But here in Butte, with its added discomfort of snow and bad weather, a man could find himself boxed in, surrounded by a force far superior than his. Whatever else he might have lacked through his loss of memory Sam Harper was quickly finding out that there were things he was still capable of. Things which appeared to be as much a part of him as the breath that kept him alive. As long as he had those skills at his fingertips he seemed likely to survive – or at least have a damn good chance of doing so. He had no way of knowing what might be in store for him once he left Butte and took off into the high country. It was wild and lonely country up there. Anything could happen. One way or another, Harper realized, he was going to find out about himself. He'd learn who he was and what he was. It might come the hard way – but he had a feeling it was the only way he knew.

4

Buck Feeney stood at the mouth of the cave and stared out morosely at the swirling snow. He hunched his shoulders against the cold, stamping his feet to keep the circulation moving. He was fed up with just sitting round and waiting. Feeney was a man used to an active life. This kind of deal didn't sit too well on his broad shoulders and it wouldn't have taken much to make him quit. It was only the money that kept him out on the bleak mountainside, cold and wet and trying without success not to think of the women back in Bannock.

'Hey, Buck, you want some more coffee?'

Feeney turned and made his way into the cave. He didn't really want any coffee. That was all he and his three companions had done since they'd made their camp here four days ago.

Drink coffee, eat, sleep, talk!

It was enough to drive a man crazy. Feeney wished something would happen. Anything. It didn't matter what – just as long as it broke the monotony.

'Another coupla days an' we'll all look like damn coffee beans,' Feeney growled, as he took the steaming mug of black liquid from Jed Cooper.

'Trouble with you, Buck, is not knowing when you're well off,' Cooper said. He was a slight man with pale, thinning hair. He had the kind of face Feeney always associated with people recovering from a bad illness. Translucent skin drawn tight over prominent bones. Large eyes that bulged from sockets seemingly too small to contain them. Contrary to his appearance, Jed Cooper was a quick-witted, humorous man, and he never wasted a chance to take a rise out of Feeney.

'Jed, you tell me once more just how good I'm doin' an' I'll kick your ass all the way up to the Canadian border,' Feeney said.

Cooper fed more wood into the flames of the fire he'd kept going from the day they had first made camp. He had discovered a natural chimney formation in the cave roof and had set about building a fire under it. Since that first day he'd made it his business to keep the fire going and to collect the wood. He'd built up a sturdy tripod arrangement over the flames and from it had hung a blackened coffeepot he kept permanently filled.

Drinking his coffee, Feeney watched Cooper's activity. He envied the man's ability to occupy himself during the long hours. His own restlessness only brought on a feeling of resentment towards Cooper.

'Christ, Jed, it's like watching an old woman!' Feeney exploded suddenly. 'For once why can't you just say shit to it all and kick that pot of damn coffee to hell!'

Cooper finished feeding the fire. He filled himself a mug of coffee and sat back against the wall of the cave. He glanced at Feeney over the rim of his mug as he drank, laughter gleaming in his eyes.

'It's not old women bothering you, Buck,' he said.

'More likely to be young ones. Like that redhead you've had your eye on. The one who works at Roche's place.'

A sullen grunt was Feeney's response. He slouched into a corner and squatted on his heels, staring into the fire. He knew the truth when it was shown to him. It was right enough. He was having a hell of a time trying to keep the memory of that red-haired little flirt out of his mind. There was too little out here to fill his mind with other thoughts, and he kept seeing her face, her eyes beckoning him, the promise of her lithe, full-breasted young body giving him an ache that wasn't about to he eased by drinking gallons of Cooper's damn coffee!

'Time Cleaver and Shannuck were getting back,' Cooper said. He climbed to his feet and went to stand at the cave mouth.

'Maybe they got lost tookin' for Benteen,' Feeney suggested. For want of something better to do he joined Cooper and they both stared out at falling snow.

The ground sloped away from the mouth of the cave. Heavy stands of timber grew on this high ground. Gracefully curved snow banks had changed the landscape, layering everything in smooth whiteness. To the west, far away, the peaks of the Bitterroot Range thrust upwards against the snow-laden sky. The normally silent land had taken on an even more desolate aspect now. The never-ending, undulating carpet of snow had given it a stark, bleak took.

'Shannuck won't get lost,' Cooper said. 'Man don't live as long as Cole Shannuck without he don't learn a few tricks.'

'Hell, Jed, he ain't God,' Feeney said acidly. 'Shannuck's like the rest of us: he can die the same as we can.'

'He's still alive when a lot of others are dead.'

Feeney spat into the snow. 'Sure he is. That's 'cause he's a lot more sneaky than the rest.'

'No! Shannuck's—'

'Shannuck's a big man! Yeah, I know!' Feeney grinned suddenly. He touched Cooper's shoulder. 'You wait on the day somebody puts a bullet through his balls. You'll see how big he is then.'

A quick smile crossed Cooper's face. 'You could be right, Buck.'

Below them a pair of riders broke out of the trees, angling their struggling horses up the slope. The riders were hunched over the necks of the horses, hats drawn tight down across their faces to protect them from the keen bite of the wind.

Cooper was the first to spot them. He turned and picked up a rifle leaning against the wall of the cave, levering a round into the breech. He moved back beside Feeney.

'You recognize them?' he asked.

Feeney shrugged. 'Looks like it could be Shannuck and Cleaver,' he said. 'Can't see too well yet.'

They waited in silence while the riders advanced to the crest of the slope. Only then were they able to recognize their companions. Cooper put aside the rifle and went out to meet them, leaving Feeney standing in the cave's mouth.

'We were getting worried, Cole,' Cooper said.

Cole Shannuck slid stiffly from his saddle. He tipped his hat back from his broad, hard-featured face. 'Times are I hate this damn country,' he said. 'Seems like it's either so hot it's like to fry a man, or so cold he's liable to freeze if he stops movin'. On top of that the whiskey tastes like cow piss and the women ain't bearable 'less they got a sack over their heads.' He handed the reins to his partner, Cleaver, then fell in beside Cooper as they made their way towards the cave. 'I hope you got some of your coffee on the boil, Jed.'

Cooper nodded. 'Way you're talkin', Cole, I'd say things ain't been goin' too well.'

A forced laugh passed Shannuck's lips. 'One thing about you, Jed: you know when to say the obvious.'

They stepped into the comparative shelter of the cave. Cooper went to the fire and poured a couple of mugs of coffee. He left one for Cleaver and handed the other to Shannuck who drank eagerly.

'God, I been needing that for a time,' Shannuck gasped. He squatted before the fire, holding his big hands over the flames.

'Where's Benteen?' Buck Feeney asked. 'Ain't he with you?'

Shannuck glanced up at him. 'Way things are I reckon Benteen's dead!'

'*Shit!*' Feeney exploded. 'No damn woman could get the drop on Benteen!'

'Who said it was the woman?' Shannuck refilled his mug.

'What happened, Cole?' Cooper asked, overriding Feeney's impatience.

'By the time we got there the Maitland woman had arrived in Butte, and left. Seems the train got slowed by the snow and couldn't go any further. Cleaver an' me did some quiet checking. We found she spent last night in one of the hotels and left Butte early this morning. By now

41

she's got a good few hours start on us.'

'Seem it was right what we heard about her,' Cooper remarked.

'Bein' sharp?' Shannuck nodded. 'Appears so.'

Feeney made an impatient sound. 'Never mind about all that crap. What about Benteen?'

Shannuck sighed. 'Persistent kind of bastard, ain't he? We went to Benteen's room. We checked Butte from one end to the other. He wasn't in town.'

'So?' Feeney demanded.

'So Benteen wasn't in town,' said a voice from his rear. It was Burt Cleaver, shaking the snow from his clothing as he stomped his way across the cave. He took the mug of coffee from Cooper and drank. 'Benteen had vanished, but his gear was in his room and his horse was at the livery.'

'Look, I ain't in the mood for this runaround,' Feeney yelled. 'How'd you know he's dead?'

'Benteen wouldn't leave town without his gear or his horse. Jesus, he'd even left that damned Winchester he fancies so much. It was up in his room with his clothes and stuff.' Shannuck held up a hand at Feeney's rising protest. 'Damnit, I know that ain't proof enough to say he's dead, but we learned something else. Seems the Maitland woman got herself a hired hand, and the pair of 'em left Butte together. She picked him up last night. Even took a room next to his. Desk clerk at the hotel told me. Real talkative kind. I showed him some dollar bills and he couldn't stop. This feller the woman hired, seems he bought a couple of horses and a heap of stuff at one of the stores. He'd been in town a while before the Maitland woman arrived. Desk clerk knew him well, but he didn't like him. Truth was he was scared of him. Can't say I blame him. . . .'

Feeney stared at him, waiting for Shannuck to continue. '*Well?*' he demanded. 'You going to tell me?'

'Go ahead, Cole,' Cleaver said. 'He's goin' to get so excited he's going to wet his pants.'

'Come on, Cole,' Feeney begged. 'Hell's teeth, man, don't make us guess!'

'Name of the feller was Sam Harper.'

Feeney didn't say anything at first, but beside him Cooper gave a low whistle. For a moment there was complete silence. Then Feeney said, '*Harper?* Sam Harper from Las Cruces way? The Harper who carried a badge?'

'He quit that a piece back,' Shannuck corrected. 'Harper ain't been wearing a badge for a time now. He rode scout for the army. Took up bounty hunting until that thing in San Felipe.'

'I recall that,' Cooper said. 'They say he caught a couple of slugs. Didn't reckon he'd be up and around again so fast.'

'So we supposed to run scared because this *might* be Harper?' Feeney scowled. He turned to Shannuck again. 'You figure because this feller Harper was in Butte, Benteen's dead?'

'Maybe you don't know much about Harper,' Shannuck said. 'I do. He's good. Better than most. He never was one to have to prove hisself. Let his gun do his talking. But he's a tough bastard. Come the day he'd shoot a man soon as look at him. Not the kind who advertised his reputation. He don't need to. Looks like Benteen didn't know that.'

'I didn't know Benteen long,' Cooper said, 'but he acted like he fancied doing things his way. You figure he tried to push things before you and Cleaver got to Butte?'

Shannuck nodded. 'Could be. Benteen always did have a quick trigger finger too.'

'He'd need more against Harper,' Cleaver said.

'So now we done deciding Benteen's dead what we going to do about the Maitland woman?' Feeney asked. 'That's why we're sittin' out in this *damn* snowstorm!'

'Don't spook yourself, Buck,' Shannuck said. He rose from where he was crouched by the fire, stretching his powerful body. He was a big man. Solid without being heavy, broad across the shoulders and with long arms. His hands were large, long fingered. 'Harper and the girl are heading for Bannock. Ain't no problem there. They're not going to get far in this weather. And it's a long ride to Bannock. Plenty of time for us to find them and deal with them.'

Feeney smiled after a moment. 'Yeah, guess you're right, Cole. Plenty of time for us.'

Beyond the mouth of the cave the swirling snow blotted out everything. The wind drove down off the high dark peaks, pushing the snow into deeper drifts.

It bent the tall trees, threatening to snap the slender trunks, and created an endless howl of sound. It was a sound that spoke of the timeless solitude of the mountains. Of the vaulted, desolate canyons. The high, grassy meadows overshadowed by the stony peaks. It was the sound of eternity. Never changing. As the mountains themselves never changed. It told the story of ages passed. It was the voice of the mountains.

5

They had made slow travel since leaving Butte. Deep snow, much of it blown into high drifts, meant they were constantly having to seek fresh ways to move ahead. Each time they stopped they lost time. Harper thought more than once that it might have been better to have waited out the storm back in Butte. He mentioned the matter to Virginia once. Her reply had been short and very much to the point – she had no intention of wasting any more time. Harper got the message and understood. She was the boss as far as he was concerned. It was her money financing the trip and paying his wages, and he had nothing better to do anyway.

Towards midday the wind began to drop. By early afternoon it had practically gone. The snow eased off too. Gradually Harper found they were making headway. Their pace didn't increase much but it was enough for them to have covered a good few miles more before darkness fell.

Virginia had produced a detailed and clearly marked map of the area just before they had left Butte. It had been sent to her by the man named Jack Bell. It showed all possible landmarks and watercourses, giving distances and even the elevations of high points. The heavy snowfall had obscured many of the landmarks but Harper found he was easily able to work out their line of travel. He realized that had she been forced to go alone, Virginia would most probably have made the trip without problems. She proved to be an excellent rider, controlling her horse with ease despite the difficult terrain. More than once she kept the animal from floundering in deep snow by sheer riding ability. Harper found, too, that her spirit was more than just verbal bravado. During the long day, riding in the face of high winds and heavy snows, Virginia never once uttered a word of complaint. Harper had felt the biting cold work its way through his thick coat, numbing his fingers despite the gloves he wore, and he knew that the physical discomfort must have affected Virginia. If it had she said nothing. She sat her saddle erect, shoulders hunched against the wind, the collar of the thick coat she wore turned up against her face. Turning to look back at her once he had allowed a smile to touch his cold lips. A picture had flashed before his eyes of Virginia standing in the door of his room back in Butte. She had put on the clothes he'd bought for her: thick shirt and a small-sized pair of Levis, a pair of fur-lined snow boots.

'Are you sure, Mr Harper?' she had asked.

'They'll keep you a sight warmer than all your fancy London fashions put together,' he'd told her. What he hadn't said was that she looked a damn sight better in the shirt and Levis than anyone he'd seen before. 'You got a good thick coat and gloves?'

Virginia had nodded. 'Yes.'

'And a hat? Something with flaps to tie down across your ears.'

She had stared at him. 'Lord, man, what are you trying

46

to make me look like?'

After a half-hour riding in the storm Virginia had stopped worrying about what she looked like. All that mattered was keeping warm, and she knew that he had been right about the kind of clothing to wear. The sort of outfit she'd been contemplating would have let her freeze very quickly.

The watery sun slid quickly out of sight. The sky darkened and black shadows etched themselves starkly against the white snow. Harper turned his horse up a long slope, aiming for the base of a high cliff above them. He had already spotted and marked out the dark opening of a cave. It wouldn't be the most desirable place to spend the night but it was going to have to do. He thought briefly of his hotel room, the bed and the comfort it offered. He forced the image from his mind. That was not for him. Not tonight. Tonight was a blanket on the hard floor of a cave somewhere in the Montana high country, with a young and beautiful English lady as his companion.

Harper slipped his cold feet from the stirrups and eased out of the saddle. He felt stiff from the ride, portions of which had been rough to say the least. He led his horse into the shelter of some timber. He off-saddled and freed the harness. From his saddle-bags he took a rope halter and slipped it over the horse's head, securing the other end to the trunk of a tree. He kicked at the snow close by the tree, exposing the grass beneath. His horse thrust its nose down at the grass straightaway.

'You need a hand?' he asked Virginia,

'No, Mr Harper.' She had followed him into the trees and her own horse was already unsaddled and tethered for the night.

47

Harper picked up his saddle and the other gear he'd dumped on the ground. With Virginia behind he made his way to the dark cave mouth.

'Shouldn't you check first?' she asked.

Harper glanced at her. 'Check?'

'Yes. I mean . . . if there's a bear or something living inside?'

He grinned. 'If there had been we would have heard by now. Ain't nothing living in there. Floor of that cave's as clean as a fresh bed sheet. No scuffmarks. No bits of food or droppings, and it doesn't go far enough back. No animal would use a little place like this.'

Virginia watched him stack his gear on the cave floor. She put her own load down. 'I must sound very green,' she said.

'Little common sense caution never hurt anyone,' Harper said. 'One thing a body can't have too much of is caution. It's good country out here, but it's a wise thing to learn its ways before you try to live with it.'

'My father used to say more or less the same thing.' For a moment her voice faltered. Then she regained control of herself. 'What can I do to help?'

'There's food and utensils in that sack. Sort them out. I'll go and get some wood for a fire.'

By the time Harper returned with a large bundle of wood Virginia had everything set out. She sat with her back against the cave wall and watched him build a fire.

'I thought you frontiersmen lit your fires by rubbing two dry sticks together,' she said lightly.

'No, ma'am,' Harper said, as he tipped his hat back and turned to her. 'This ain't exactly the frontier, and seeing how all that stick rubbing tended to be a darn nuisance, we got this clever feller to invent the match.'

He took out the small box and rattled it for her. Then he bent to his task and shortly had the fire burning.

Virginia smiled, her eyes shining in the bright flames rising from the pile of wood. She watched the growing flames, her gaze following the red sparks which writhed up into the dark sky.

'Couldn't the fire be seen from a long way off?' she asked suddenly.

Harper had been waiting for that question. 'Yes, ma'am. It can be seen. And if that feller back in Butte had friends we might not be alone up here tonight. If that's so *and* they're around we'll know soon enough. We've left a pretty clear trail through the snow since the storm quit. Won't take a genius to work out the route we've been taking. Depends how close they are. One thing they won't be doing is riding around in the dark. In these conditions night riding would be suicide. But I don't count on that being the end of the matter. Man doesn't have to depend on a horse. He could come on foot – or *they* could. So lighting a fire doesn't make much difference. If they want us they'll find us. All we can do is wait. Might as well be comfortable while we do that waiting.'

'And eat I hope,' Virginia said.

Harper sliced some of the salted bacon he'd brought. He passed it to Virginia who dropped it into the small frying pan wedged over the flames. Soon the aroma of fried bacon drifted up into the dark sky. Harper crushed some coffee beans, filled the coffee pot with water from his canteen and tossed in the beans, adding a little salt to the concoction. He put the pot over the flames, took his rifle and went to collect more wood. He wanted to keep the fire going during the long night and knew that there was the possibility of the snowstorm coming again.

They ate the bacon with hard biscuits, washing it down with cups of hot, black coffee. Both of them had good appetites from the day's ride. Harper found he was watching Virginia Maitland closely, surprised at the way she accepted the primitive conditions they were forced to put up with. She was obviously a young woman of remarkable talents.

'Not up to the standard you're used to, but it's the best we'll get out here,' he found himself telling her.

Virginia smiled at him. 'If I told you some of the things I've eaten, Mr Harper, I think you would be rather surprised. When my father was alive he often took me along on hunting trips. I have camped out in the African bush and the jungles of India.'

'Wouldn't you have preferred a life at home? Husband? Children?'

'Now you are asking personal questions, Mr Harper. But I don't mind answering. If the opportunity had come along I suppose I would have been content. The circumstances, however, have never presented themselves. Somehow my life has always been full of challenges. Enough to give me satisfaction. I have never deliberately tried to dissuade the attentions of the men I have known. Far from it. Even so here I am, and here you are, Mr Harper.' There was a long moment of silence while Virginia fixed her gaze on his shadowed face. 'You still appear to be reluctant to talk about yourself. Contrary to your rules concerning a man's business being his own, I am still curious to know more about you.'

Harper leaned forward to fill his coffee cup. Her directness had caught him off balance. He had left himself open to her questions by his own inquisitive impulse. Whichever way he turned now she would be there, waiting for his answer. The trouble was what did he tell her? She knew his name and had seen for herself his ability to handle a violent situation. He didn't know much more himself. Too much of his personality still lay out of reach.

'Couple of months back,' he began, searching for the words he needed, 'I had an accident while I was doing a job. I took a couple of bullets. One that like to bust open my skull. It was down San Felipe way. I was out of it for a fair few weeks.'

'Are you recovered well enough now?'

'I know my name and where I am. That's just about as much as *you* know about me,' Harper said, watching for her reaction.

Virginia put down her cup. 'You have no memory of your past? Where you come from, or what you've done?'

'That's what everybody keeps telling me. Only reason I know what happened was I heard it from the people back in San Felipe. Seems I was on a bounty hunt. Trailing a trio of renegades wanted by the law. Appears I caught up with 'em in San Felipe and we went at it. They ended up dead but not before they put their lead in me.'

'It appears I owe you an apology, Mr Harper,' Virginia said. 'I've been thinking you were just being unsociable and all the time there was nothing you had to tell me.'

'Maybe I should have told you back in Butte.' Harper grinned. ' 'Course you probably wouldn't have given me the job if you'd known.'

'I offered you the job on the basis of what I saw in Butte. And I don't think I judged wrongly.'

'Now you know what I did for a living mebbe you want to change your mind.'

Virginia shook her head. 'I doubt that very much, Mr Harper. You proved yourself to me back in Butte and you certainly appear competent out here.'

'You still want to carry on?'

'Of course. Mr Harper, you may have lost your memory but you certainly haven't lost whatever ability you possess. I am confident that ability will see us through to Bannock.'

'We'll be starting early. Best if you get as much rest as you can.'

Virginia nodded. She moved away from the fire and unrolled her blankets. She busied herself spreading them on the floor of the cave.

'Mr Harper, you will wake me? If there is any trouble, I mean.'

'If we have trouble, ma'am, I doubt there'll be any need to wake you. You'll hear it.' Harper fed more wood to the fire. 'But if it'll help you sleep easier – don't fret. I'll let you know if there's a need.'

'Thank you, Mr Harper.'

Finishing his coffee, Harper buttoned his coat, picked up his rifle and stepped outside the cave. He took a walk to where the horses were tethered. They lifted their heads as he approached, but once they recognized him they went back to their grazing. Circling away from the horses, Harper walked some distance away from the cave. He stopped when he figured he'd gone far enough. He could see the fire blazing just outside the cave. It threw plenty of light across the white slope fronting the cave. Luckily there was no cover within a couple of hundred feet of the cave. As long as he kept the fire going nobody was liable to sneak up on them, and at least they would stay reasonably warm. No point in the pair of them freezing to death.

He retraced his steps back to the cave. Kicking the snow from his boots, Harper picked up his blankets and found himself a spot at the cave mouth. He draped the blankets round his shoulders, filled himself a cup of steaming coffee and settled his back against the stone behind him. He glanced across at Virginia's still form, and for a fleeting second found himself wondering what it would be like to be under the blankets with her. He felt his body stir, felt the swelling warmth in his groin, and called himself every kind of a fool to allow himself to harbour such thoughts at such a time. He had a long night ahead. No time to let himself get all hot and bothered by his imagination. He knew he'd do better concentrating on the job in hand. He would have felt easier in his mind if he'd known from the start the kind of opposition he might be up against.

He was literally in the dark over the matter. There could be a dozen of them out there. Or two dozen. Then again none at all. His only course was to keep his eyes open and be ready if and when something did happen.

Much later, as he jerked his cold-stiffened body into movement, reaching to refill his cup with more coffee, he noticed the first flakes of a fresh fall of snow. Within a few minutes the fall had become heavy. Harper watched it with mixed feelings. It might make the job of any pursuers that much more difficult, but it wasn't going to do anything to ease his own problems.

6

Running had been the only way out left to Jack Bell.

He was no coward. Nor a fool. He was simply a man who had come to realize how close to death he was. True to his stubborn nature he had kept on working, doing what he could to find out who was behind the mine's troubles. The early warnings he'd received to stop his investigations had rolled off Jack Bell's back as water off a duck. Then two attempts on his life had finally etched the message into his mind, and he suddenly became aware he was in the most difficult position of his life. Bell had been in the mining business since his seventeenth birthday. It was a hard life and a man needed to be just as hard to stay alive. Jack Bell had been in tight corners before. He had survived cave-ins, explosions and any number of natural calamities. He had faced human problems too and had always walked away unhurt. But this time he realized the only way he was going to stay alive was by getting clear of Bannock.

The final warning had been direct and designed to silence him for good. Bell had almost walked into the set-up blind, but a moment of sheer good luck had come his way, allowing Bell not only finally to identify the mine fore-man he had suspected of being behind the betrayal, but had exposed the man he was conspiring with. When the two had parted company, laying the final seeds of the trap for Bell, he had gone after the treacherous foreman and had confronted him. The man had panicked at his exposure and the realization his plan was not going to work. In his panic he had gone for Bell, striking at him with a knife. The struggle had been short and had ended with Bell standing over the only man he had ever killed, still with the other man's knife in his hand.

Unsure who else he could trust, Bell had decided it was time to get out. He needed to get clear of the mine, allowing himself the chance of telegraphing Virginia Maitland and warning her that the threat against the mine was real.

He had ridden out while the storm raged about him. The hostile elements held no fear for him. Jack Bell knew the country and he knew how to survive. He figured the chance worth taking.

He hadn't counted on the man named Puma, the one he had seen with the now dead foreman. Bell had heard the name before. A silent, menacing figure, known simply by the one name – Puma. A killer by trade and by choice, Puma was a man apart from all others. He was part white, part Indian, and he was all bad. Jack Belt had known Puma's kind before. They hired out for money when someone needed a killing done. They were hated and feared. Despised by those who hired them as well as those they went against. But no man ever spoke openly against men like Puma. Unless they had tired of life. Jack Bell had no cause to like Puma but he had sense enough to respect the man's skill, repellant as it was. He knew his deadly reputation and he also knew that the man had a long record of successful kills – and he had never been caught.

Bell became aware of Puma's presence towards the end of the first day out from the mine. The snowstorm had eased off towards the end of the afternoon. The brutal wind had dropped and the snow also lightened. It was as he had taken his weary horse over the crest of a snow-layered slope, turning in the saddle to check his back trail.

And for the first time he saw the motionless figure on the pale, dun-coloured horse. Despite the distance, and despite the glare of the snow, Jack Bell knew who the lone rider was. Only one man would trail another so openly, making no attempt to conceal himself. It was the supreme confidence of the professional man-hunter. The inborn skill of the killer breed. It could only be one man.

It could only be Puma.

The low temperature had nothing to do with the icy clutch of fear twisting Jack Belt's insides. He had looked on the man named Puma and he had felt the landscape lurch with sickening force. Bell figured he had a right to be afraid. He considered himself as tough as the next man but against someone like Puma he was a novice. He hadn't grown up with a gun in his hand, seeking the lives of others, spilling blood for money. It took a special kind of man to do that – a man like Puma – and only a damn fool would pretend there was no need for concern.

Bell had spurred his horse on, ignoring his earlier caution. He drove the rapidly tiring animal over the undulating, hilly landscape. Somewhere at the back of his mind he knew he was doing wrong. He was risking his own neck as well as the horse's. But he wanted to get some distance between himself and Puma.

The rifle shot cleaved the air with a crisp, echoing crack. Belt felt his horse shudder. The animal made a shrill sound. Its head dropped and a red spray fountained from its nostrils, fading to a pale pink as it merged with the snow. Bell hauled up on the reins, knowing it was a futile gesture. He kicked his feet from the stirrups and, as his stricken horse stumbled to its knees, he rolled from the saddle. He made a grab for the sheathed rifle fastened to the saddle. His cold fingers failed to get a grip. The thick snow cushioned his fall. He skidded forward on his knees, struggling to control his movements, and cursing his own stupidity at letting himself be taken so easily. As he turned back towards his horse, keeping as low as possible, he saw that he'd lost the rifle. The dying horse had fallen on the gun, pinning it beneath its solid bulk. Bell realized too that there was no time to try and loosen the blanket roll or the food pack tied behind the saddle. If he wanted to stay alive he was going to have to do it with what he was carrying.

He threw a quick glance around, his eyes seeking the closest cover. Over to his left, but at least a hundred yards away lay tangled brush. There was nothing closer. Bell angled away from his horse, his numb fingers jerking at the buttons of his thick coat. A short-barrelled .44-40 Colt handgun lay in a holster against his right hip and Bell wanted the weapon in his hand.

He heard the second shot!

A stunning blow caught him in the left shoulder, spinning him off his feet and throwing him face down in the snow. The sudden flare of pain made him cry out. He felt the sharp bite of snow against his face, icy against his lips. Bell struggled upright, ignoring the sickening pain flaring in his shattered shoulder. His left arm dangled uselessly at his side. The bullet had gone right through, bursting out of the front of his coat. A bloody mess of shredded cloth and lacerated flesh marked the coat. He could feet hot blood streaming down his arm and, as he ran, he left a spatter of pink on the white snow.

This time he didn't bother about attempting to keep low. He just ran. Jerking open his coat, he yanked out the heavy revolver, gripping the hard butt tightly. He didn't care that the weapon was only useful at short range. The feel of the weapon gave him comfort, and right then it was important to him.

He missed his footing and crashed face down in the snow. Pain tore through his shoulder and he bit his lip to keep from crying out. This time his face scraped against something hard beneath the soft snow, something which tore at his flesh. Bell twisted over onto his back, dragging himself up off the ground. He stood for a moment, his breath steaming from his mouth in frosty clouds. He blinked his eyes against the glare of the snow, staring at the dark, wavering shape some distance off. He was too far away to see clearly but he knew who it was. A hot flush of anger rose in him and he lifted the hand holding the revolver, his thumb dragging back on the hammer. Then he lowered the gun, his anger abating. He would only waste a bullet. His target was too far away. And would stay that way. The man named Puma was no fool. He wouldn't allow himself to be drawn into the range of Bell's gun. Puma carried a long-range rifle. He could stay at a safe distance and put a bullet into Bell just when he wanted to.

Jack Bell stared at the silent rider. Damn the man. He was like some animal; lusting after blood; killing without emotion – for no more than a handful of dollar bills.

Aware suddenly of his exposed position Bell broke into

a stumbling run, hampered by the clinging snow. He slipped and slid across the open ground, closing the gap between himself and the distant brush. With every passing second he expected to hear the vicious crack of Puma's rifle. He was yards off the brush when the anticipated shot came. It struck the snow inches from his left foot, and Bell knew he'd been given a momentary reprieve. He found himself counting the seconds as he visualized Puma working the lever of the rifle, pushing another shell into the chamber, lifting and aiming, his finger easing back on the trigger.

Bell saw the tangled mass of brush ahead and threw himself forward. Dimly he heard the crash of the shot. Something hot burned its way across his right hip, clipping bone, and spinning him helplessly. He smashed through the brush, rolling as he hit the hard ground beneath. Gasping air into his burning lungs Jack Bell crawled deeper into the brush. He clenched his teeth against the pain of his wounds and kept moving. Puma would still be looking for him. The half-breed wasn't the type to quit. He wouldn't give up the hunt until one of them was dead, Bell knew that and he didn't intend being the one to die. He still had his revolver clutched in his right hand. If the opportunity arose he'd use the gun on Puma without hesitation.

Somewhere far behind him he heard a horse snort. The thick brush crackled and snapped as a heavy bulk forced its way through. Bell peered through the tangled brush ahead. He had no idea in which direction he was moving. Not that it made much difference. He was only interested in getting some distance between himself and Puma. He needed time to rest. Time to tend to his wounds if he was able.

He felt the soft snow beneath him slide away. For a moment he didn't understand what was happening. He was too late by the time realization came to him. He caught a glimpse of the white slope below him, dropping away forever it seemed. Then there was no more time for anything. He was falling, his body twisting as it dropped into space. After a time his body struck something and he began to slide. More than once hard objects slammed against his body, sharp things tore at his clothing and at his flesh. Oddly he felt little pain. He became aware too that there was an odd silence. He couldn't even hear his own breathing. His body fell into open space again, then almost as abruptly he came into hard contact with the slope. The impact drove the breath from his body. He knew that he had lost his grip on the revolver. But he realized that it didn't matter any more. Nothing mattered.

His downward flight was stopped. Bell slammed against hard ground. The impact numbed him. He lay barely conscious, his body trembling, throbbing with terrible pain. He tried to lift his head but only succeeded in moving it slightly. He tasted blood in his mouth. There was a sudden heavy roaring sound in his ears. He felt a rush of sickness and his head flopped back onto the snow. He felt all physical sensation slip away. Darkness overtook him. Complete and utter darkness. Bell didn't try to resist. He let himself slide into the black maw of unconsciousness.

7

'*What do you think these people are after?*'

Harper had asked the question while they'd been eating breakfast. He had caught Virginia's slight shrug.

'I can only guess, Mr Harper. It might simply be an attempt to put the Maitland mines out of business. There are a number of rival companies who certainly wouldn't shed any tears if Maitland Copper ceased to operate. Then it could be union trouble. Militant union groups have been known to go to extreme measures to get what they want.'

'Even though you told me your father had always dealt fairly with his workers?'

Virginia smiled. 'Unfortunately there are those in the unions who are more interested in obtaining a stronger hold on a company than they are in the fact that the workers are already getting a fair deal.'

'Has your company issued shares?'

'Certainly. I hold the majority but there is a substantial stock issue. An extremely profitable issue too.'

'But it has been known for stockholders to sell and then the issuing company finds itself in trouble?'

'By all means, Mr Harper. The shares of Maitland Copper

are only as good as the company which brought them into being. If the company goes through hard times the shares reflect that difficulty.'

'The price drops and a lot of shares can be bought cheaply?'

'Mr Harper, you've given me food for *thought* as well as food for my stomach.' Virginia put down her empty plate. 'Perhaps Jack Bell will be able to tell us more.'

Within an hour they had cleared camp, saddled the horses and moved out. The snow was still falling but they could see their way clearly. A gentle wind gusted down off the higher peaks, gathering dusty coils of snow. The unmarked trail they were following led higher onto the forested slopes. Harper unsheathed his rifle, preferring to have the weapon out and ready. He let his horse pick its way across the undulating blanket of snow, using his eyes to scan the surrounding heights, the dark lines of trees. There were, he realized, a damn lot of places where a man could hide. Maybe too many. But there was no safer way to get where they were going.

Towards the middle of the morning they were moving along the floor of a long valley. Steep slopes, rippled by drifted snow, reared up on either side. Harper was beginning to feel hemmed in, and there was the hint of an itchy spot between his shoulders. It could have been the product of an over-active imagination. On the other hand. . . .

'*Mr Harper.*'

Harper reined in hard, jerking his horse about. He threw a quick glance towards Virginia. Her voice had been low, controlled, yet urgent, and even now she kept a grip on her emotions.

'I saw a rider. On the top of the slope. To the right.'

Harper twisted his body, searching the uneven line of the rim above them. He couldn't see anything. No movement. No shape out of place.

'Just one?' he asked.

Virginia nodded. 'Yes.' She stared at him for a moment. 'I didn't imagine it, Mr Harper,' she added, her tone edged with ice.

'Take it easy. I'm not doubting you.'

'Sorry.'

Harper nodded. 'Just keep looking,' he said.

There was no reply from Virginia. Harper saw that she was looking over his shoulder. By the look in her eyes she'd seen something. He saw the colour drain from her cheeks. Harper hauled himself round in his saddle, swinging his rifle ahead of him, not certain what he was about to face.

For a moment he thought his eyes were playing tricks on him. He appeared to be looking at a living snowman. A shuffling, slow-moving creature formed from the very snow and ice around them. But then he realized that it was a man. Covered in crusted, frozen snow that had formed itself to the body and the face, clinging to the very features. He saw, too, the brownish stains showing through the crusted white.

Blood!

As Harper slid from his saddle, the stumbling figure toppled forward. First to its knees and then face down in the snow. Harper moved to where the figure lay. He grasped a near-rigid arm and gently rolled the figure over. He sensed Virginia kneeling on the other side, her slender fingers brushing iced snow away from the blistered face. Harper could hear the man's laboured breathing now, a harsh, ragged sound.

'Looks like he's been out all night,' Harper said. He could see the dark discoloration of the flesh of the hands. *Frostbite.* There was nothing they could do for that. He wondered who the poor bastard was? His question was answered by the gasp coming from Virginia.

'What's wrong?'

Tears gleamed in her eyes as she looked across at him. 'It's Jack Bell.'

Harper stood up, moving away from Virginia and the man called Bell.

He went to his horse and jerked his blanket roll free, tossing it towards Virginia. She opened the blankets and pulled them across Bell's body. It was a futile gesture. Harper knew it and he was sure that Virginia realized the hopelessness of it.

'Isn't there anything we can do for him?' she asked.

Harper shook his head. 'I don't think he'll last much longer. It's a hell of a thing to say, ma'am, but there's no other way to say it.'

'Poor Jack. I feel so bad just sitting here and not doing anything.'

As sorry as he was for Bell, Harper's main concern was his and Virginia's safety. They were in a bad position on the valley floor. It was too exposed, lacking in any real protective cover.

'What's going on, Mr Harper?' Virginia's voice revealed her confusion. 'First that man tries to kill you and now this. I don't understand.'

'I figure we'll find that out in Bannock.' Harper expressed his feelings by his sharp reply, ignoring Virginia's surprised reaction. He wasn't overly concerned about her feelings at that precise moment. Their situation didn't allow time for the finer points of etiquette.

Neither Harper or Virginia Maitland had the chance to continue the conversation. A group of horsemen had showed on the far rim of the valley. Harper watched them hesitate for a moment and then push their horses on down the slope. They were too far away for him to recognize faces, and though he had no knowledge of them Harper didn't intend waiting for them to get any closer. He grabbed up the reins of their horses, yanking the motionless animals out of their lethargy.

'*Let's go,*' he snapped.

Virginia swung her head round, cheeks flaring with colour at his impatient tone. About to comment on his manner she stayed silent as her eyes focused on the distant riders. Her eyes settled on Harper's face, noting the hardness in his features. She stood up and took the reins of her horse.

'*What about. . . ?*'

Harper had jammed his rifle back in its sheath. For a moment he seemed about to argue. Then his shoulders sagged in resignation. Without a word he bent over Jack Bell, took hold of the unconscious man's coat and hauled him up off the ground. Grunting with the effort he humped Bell across his saddle.

'Satisfied?' he asked, his voice brittle with agitation.

Virginia nodded. 'Thank you, Mr Harper.'

'Then get your butt in that damn saddle and let's get the hell out of here.'

Harper's horse balked at having to carry a double load. It changed its mind after Harper gave it a couple of brutal punches between the ears. Harper owed his life to the tenacity of horses he'd had in the past and he wasn't too keen on hard treatment, but horses, like people, sometimes had to be shaken out of themselves. This was one of those times.

They moved along the valley floor, their speed reduced by the drifted snow. Virginia rode ahead of Harper, struggling to keep her mount moving. The animal had taken a dislike to the sudden departure and fought against her urging it on. Harper was faring no better. Coupled with trying to maintain a steady pace, he was hampered by the need to keep Jack Bell from slipping from his saddle and also by trying to keep an eye on the bunch of riders. It seemed to Harper that their position had become more than a little difficult.

The flat sound of a rifle cut through the near silence. The bullet fell yards short, kicking up a geyser of powdered snow. Other shots followed, moving progressively closer as the riflemen found the range. Harper searched the immediate area, seeking anything which might give them a way out of the valley. He knew almost from the start that nothing was going to show. Either they rode on until they reached the natural end of the valley, or they took their horses up the snow-covered slopes. Neither way held much comfort.

The whip crack slam of a bullet only inches from Virginia's horse caused the animal to panic. Despite Virginia's strong handling, it fought against the reins, sidestepping wildly. Harper swore angrily. That was all they needed. He drove his own horse up alongside, grabbing at the reins of Virginia's animal. He caught a quick glimpse of her white face as she glanced at him. Harper dragged the struggling horse's head round, keeping his own mount's body pressed hard against that of the skittish horse. All the time he was increasingly aware of the approach of the group of riders.

The horse under Harper shuddered. A shrill sound burst from it. Harper felt it stumble as its hindquarters gave. Harper slid his feet from the stirrups, jumping to the ground as the horse went down. It lay kicking, eyes rolling, blood streaming from a dark hole in its side.

'*Get down,*' Harper yelled. He reached up and caught Virginia's arm, dragging her out of the saddle. He turned away from her then, ignoring the fact that she had landed face down in the snow. With the knowledge that time was slipping away too quickly, Harper crouched by his horse, his cold fingers loosening the thongs holding his saddlebags secure. He dragged the bags free, the canteen, then yanked at the sack holding the food.

'*Take them!*' he yelled over his shoulder at Virginia, shoving the things to his rear. Raising his head above the still trembling bulk of the horse Harper snatched his rifle from its sheath. He threw a quick glance across the valley floor towards the advancing riders. The riders, four of them, had reached the base of the slope and were moving along the level ground. They had spread out in a ragged line abreast, and they seemed to be taking their time. Harper watched them, narrowing his eyes against the falling snow.

'Mr Harper!'

'Yeah?'

Virginia's voice dropped to a whisper. 'I think Jack is dead.'

Harper sighed. 'Make sure one way or the other. We might have to get out of here fast.'

'How?'

There was no reply. Harper had leaned forward across the downed horse, levelling his rifle. He held still for a moment then pulled the trigger. The rifle spat a lance of flame and powdersmoke. Virginia's eyes were drawn towards the distant horsemen. She felt her body stiffen with shock as one of the riders lurched sideways in his saddle. For a second, Virginia thought the man would fall but he made a supreme effort and dragged himself upright again. He sat straight for a moment then sagged forward across his horse's neck. There was a long moment of stillness, broken when another of the riders returned Harper's shot. A number of bullets struck the ground around the downed horse. Virginia threw herself to the ground, trembling. When she lifted her head again she saw that the four riders had drawn off a way and were sitting watching. It was almost as if they were waiting for something to happen.

'Ma'am, you all right?'

Virginia gathered herself. She felt cold, almost sick. She couldn't trust her voice so she answered Harper's question with a quick nod. She watched him draw away from the shot horse, saw him bend over Jack Bell's still body. Only now did she notice the fresh blood marking Bell's shoulder, more on his hip. She found herself unable to look at his face.

'He's dead,' Harper said.

He didn't wait for any reaction from Virginia. He was more concerned with the living. Twisting round he peered through the curtain of falling snow and out across the valley floor. The four riders were still in the same place. One of them was at the side of the one Harper had shot, doing something to the man's shoulder.

Harper turned about, staring up the steep slope behind them. It was a fair way to the top, and no way of telling what lay beyond. For a brief moment he wondered if he wasn't crazy in what he was contemplating. There was probably a degree of insanity in his intention, but there was little else they could do. They had four armed men on their heels, only one horse – which had already wandered away from them he noticed with irritation – and nowhere to go except up that damned slope. On foot too, he realized sourly. He thought back to that moment in Butte when he'd left the comforting warmth of that restaurant to follow Virginia Maitland. He'd done it on impulse, sure that she was going to have some kind of trouble, and because of his own boredom he'd involved himself in her business. Maybe that crack on the head had done more than just take away his memory. It looked as if it might have impaired his judgement because he'd really picked a poor hand this time.

'Well, Mr Harper, what do we do? Sit here and freeze.'

He stared at her. Virginia's voice trembled as she spoke and her face looked ghastly pale. But he sensed the strength behind the momentary fear.

'No, ma'am,' he said. He crawled towards her, picking up the saddle-bags he'd dumped in the snow and draping them over his shoulder. 'Can you manage that sack and the canteen?'

Virginia nodded.

'I'm only going to get a chance to say this once, so you listen. When I give the word, we make a run up that slope. You go first and you keep going. If you fall down get up and keep going. Never mind about me. Just keep movin'. Understand?'

'Yes, Mr Harper, I understand.'

'There's liable to be some shooting. I ain't expecting it to be easy for you but try not to pay any attention. Just keep goin'. No matter what you hear. *Right?*'

Her wide-eyed stare was disconcerting. Harper realized she was probably scared witless. He muttered something unintelligible under his breath and reached out to pat her hand.

A shot rang out. Nearby, a horse screamed in pain. Harper jerked his head round and saw Virginia's go down in a threshing heap, pink stains in the snow.

'*No.*'

Virginia's cry fed his anger, and Harper rose to one knee. He lifted his rifle and drove a couple of shots at the distant riders. His aim was off and the bullets struck the snow a few feet short. One of the riders found himself struggling to control a frightened animal. The horse reared suddenly, dumping the rider in the snow.

The distraction his shots caused would only be brief, Harper knew. Even so those few seconds could be worth a lot. He rolled back to where Virginia crouched.

'Now,' he said. 'Let's go.'

She didn't hesitate. Picking up the sack of food and canteen, Virginia rose to her feet and ran. Stumbling and slipping, floundering in the drifted snow, she made for the slope. Harper followed, thumbing fresh shells into the breech of his rifle. He had a feeling he was going to be needing it.

He'd only just reached the base of the slope when the first shots sounded. A bullet thumped into the ground close to his left. Another plucked at his coat. Harper turned and raised his rifle. He could see the four riders coming across the level ground, firing as they came. They were at a disadvantage. Shooting from the back of a running horse wasn't the best way to hit a target. Harper picked the lead rider. Just as he touched the trigger he became aware that it was the man he'd shot earlier. This time it *was* a killing shot. The bullet took the man in the chest, rolling him off the back of his horse and dumping him face down in the snow. Shifting his aim Harper fired twice more. One bullet missed. The last one dropped a running horse, spilling the rider out of the saddle. The man slid for yards across the hard ground before he was able to control his movements. He finally gained his feet and scrambled to get control of the horse belonging to the man Harper had shot out of the saddle. He hauled himself onto the animal and reined it about. All three riders separated, falling back out of range, though they returned Harper's fire with a fusillade of wasted shots.

Facing about, Harper moved on up the slope. He could see Virginia above him. She appeared to be doing as he'd suggested, paying no mind to what was taking place below.

The crack of a rifle reminded Harper of the men still able to use their guns. He dug in his toes, thrusting himself forward. The thick snow made moving difficult. Harper found he was often sliding back a foot for every two he moved forward. Despite the cold he began to sweat. His clothing stuck to his body. More shots sounded. Bullets drove into the slope around him. Then Harper heard a cry. He looked up to where Virginia had fallen to her knees. A cold sweat beaded his face as he struggled towards her. By the time he reached her, Virginia was pushing to her feet.

'You hurt?' he asked brusquely.

She gave him one of her spirited looks. 'I'll manage, Mr Harper. Thank you for your concern.' She got to her feet and moved on. Harper caught a glimpse of blood staining the sleeve of her coat just below her left elbow.

He turned again to look down on the valley floor. The remaining three riders were urging their mounts up the slope. Harper loosed off three quick shots and saw them scatter, struggling to control panicked horses.

The rest of the journey up the valley side took place in fits and starts. Harper took every opportunity to keep the three riders at a safe distance. He used the advantage of the steep slope, and by the time he and Virginia had pulled themselves over the crest of the slope, the three riders had only managed to gain the first few yards of the climb.

Harper dropped to his knees beside Virginia. They were both breathing hard, their bodies aching from the effort of dragging themselves up the steep slope. Even during the brief rest Harper took time to reload his rifle. He became aware of Virginia's close observance.

'I believe, Mr Harper, that this kind of situation is not new to you,' she said. She watched the sure way his fingers fed fresh shells into the rifle. He was a man to whom guns were as natural as brushes to an artist. In a way that was how she saw him. He was an artist but his art was that of killing!

8

Harper thrust a final shell into his rifle and worked the lever. He glanced across to where Virginia had slumped in the snow, her hand cupped over the bloodstained sleeve of her coat. Her head lifted and she stared at him, her eyes reflecting the jumbled thoughts she carried in her mind.

'Is this really happening, Mr Harper?' she asked. Her voice held a dull near-panic tone. 'It's like some night-mare: Jack Bell dead; armed men chasing us; killing. Tell me how this can happen!'

'Ain't uncommon out here,' Harper said. 'You're not in England now. Country's wild and so are its ways.' He climbed to his feet. 'When we got the time I'll discuss it with you. Best thing we can do right now is get the hell away from here. I stopped one of those fellers but there're still three more. I don't figure they'll feel like discussing anything either.'

Virginia stood up, trailing the food sack and canteen in the snow. Standing before Harper she appeared small and childlike in her bulky clothes. She waited for him to tell her what to do.

'First chance we have to rest I'll look at that arm,' Harper said.

Virginia nodded. 'Thank you, Mr Harper.'

He pointed out across the snowy landscape. 'We'll go that way,' he said. 'Looks as if we'll have some cover anyway. And the name's Sam,' he added. 'Time we dropped this formal stuff.'

A quick smile ghosted across Virginia's pale face but it was lost to Sam Harper. He had already turned away, trudging doggedly across the white, unmarked snow. Virginia shrugged and followed him.

They moved slowly away from the valley edge, their passage taking them towards a straggling line of trees that marched up a long slope. Once in amongst the trees they were able to move a little faster. The snow wasn't as deep in amongst the timber. It was dark, deep shadows cutting across their path. It seemed quieter too. The dense timber and the soft earth beneath the snow helped to silence the sound of their movement. Once or twice the cathedral hush was broken by the hissing sound of layered snow falling from the upper branches of tall trees. The first time it happened Virginia felt herself tense up, her body aching with a near-paralyzing shock.

As they started to work their way up the slope, huge, tumbled boulders barred their way, looming grey and white among the timber. Thick, tangled masses of fern and wild thorn grew over and around the rocks, making the way through a painful process. Virginia found herself accepting each new difficulty as it came, without complaint, even to herself. She just had no energy, or desire to make any protest against this situation. Incredible as it was, in complete contrast to her normal

74

way of life, it didn't seem to matter. She was here, she was involved, and the only way to get herself out was by seeing it through to its conclusion – whatever that might be.

Without warning, Harper turned about. His gaunt face held a bitter expression and Virginia heard him swear softly as he went on by her. As she turned herself, casting her gaze back along the way they'd come, she saw the dark shapes of mounted men moving through the timber below.

'Keep moving,' Harper told her. 'And stay low if you can.' He didn't look to see if she'd done as he'd told her. His eyes were fixed on the three riders. A cold gleam came into his eyes as he watched the trio split up, each man making his own trail. They were getting smart. Making it harder for him to watch them all. Harper sank down behind a flat slab of stone, resting his rifle across the top. He let the three riders come on. Minutes slid by. Harper didn't move until he could hear the closest of the riders.

The soft creak of leather. Metallic chinks from loose harness. He edged along the rock, twisting his body so that he would be able to see the rider.

A white flurry of dislodged snow spumed up off the ground as the rider forced his horse up over a thick hummock. Harper stood upright, lifting his rifle and firing all in the same movement. He saw his bullet hit. The rider's head snapped back, a burst of red misting the air. He fell off his horse, landing on the back of his neck, but he was dead before he touched the ground. His limp body slid partway back down the slope, leaving a sticky smear of blood and brains in the white snow.

Harper had already moved off up the slope. He could

see Virginia's dark shape ahead of him. Breathing hard, Harper closed the distance between them. He was yards away when he sensed movement in the timber off to his left. He jerked that way, swinging up the rifle. He knew before he pulled the trigger that he was too late. The rider, leaning over his horse's neck, gun thrust forward, had a face Harper felt he knew. He didn't know from where or when – he just had a memory of having seen the man before.

He heard the sound of the shot. Something hit him in the chest, high up and Harper went over backwards. He landed hard, his shoulders taking most of the impact. A numbing pain was spreading across his chest. Harper fought to gain his feet. He struggled over onto his knees. He could hear the sound of the rider's horse close behind him. Harper cursed weakly. His movements were slow, clumsy, even though his mind was active, racing ahead. He gained his feet, turning to face the oncoming rider. Out of the corner of one eye he spotted another horseman angling across the timbered slope.

He refused to accept defeat. He yanked the rifle up from his hip with an extreme effort, pulling the trigger as it ranged in on the looming horsemen. There was another shot – and a searing flash of pain that burned into his very brain. Harper screamed against the agony. It was a sound-less scream. Harper couldn't hear it. He couldn't see or feel sensation.

He didn't feel the bruising his body received as it fell, twisting across the slope before it dropped over the edge of a rock-strewn gully. Luckily he was unconscious to the pain as he went down the steep side of the gully, smashing to a dead stop amongst the tangle of fern and thorn at the bottom. Disturbed snow followed his downward passage, piling up over his body. Once the small avalanche of snow had ceased, there was no sign of movement in the gully bottom. . . .

9

Stubbornly ignoring the protests of his bruised and lacerated body, Sam Harper clawed his way out of the deep,
rock-strewn gully. Inch by inch, his raw fingers leaving
bloody marks on everything he touched. He finally rolled
himself over the crest of the slope where he lay panting,
his battered face pressed against the cold snow. There was
a nagging ache threatening to burst his skull apart and
with every breath a savage pain ripped across his chest. He
knew he was a fool to go on without rest. He had been
lucky to climb out of that gully. He realized he'd been
closer to death than he'd a right to step away from.
Waking into a world of pain, his snow-covered body half
frozen, Harper had quickly become aware of his close
escape. He hadn't deliberated over the matter for very
long. His position was particularly fraught with danger.
Initially he had needed to get himself up off the ground.
To draw life and movement back into his limbs. It had
taken time. His first attempt to climb to his feet had
reduced him to a trembling hulk, his very being screaming
for release from the hurt. After that he'd taken things at a
gentler pace, ignoring the insistent voice which kept
reminding him of Virginia. He was unable to forget her,

and he kept asking himself the same questions over and over.

Where was she?

How was she?

What had happened to her since he'd been shot? The need to know the answer was the driving force helping him to make the long climb out of the gully. Lurking on the fringes of his conscious thought was the knowledge of one possibility: that Virginia might be dead. Already he had been shown the ruthless lengths to which her pursuers would go. The deliberate hunting of Virginia and himself. The killing of Jack Bell. He needed little more to convince him.

The image of Virginia, possibly lying dead on some distant slope of the mountains, came to him with startling clarity. Harper dragged himself upright and stared around, his eyes searching the snow for tracks. It had stopped snowing during the time he'd been in the gully. By the condition of the light and the long shadows beginning to stalk across the landscape, he judged it to be close to the end of the day. He realized that he must have been unconscious for four or five hours. It was a long time. *Too long?* He refused to allow himself to become dismayed at the thought.

He raised a hand to rub his chest as a stab of pain caused him to gasp. He'd been surprised, and relieved, to find no bullet wound where he'd been hit. The explanation revealed itself to be lying in the snow at his feet. His rifle with its breechblock twisted out of shape. He remembered the sound of the shot, then the stunning burst of pain. The bullet had struck his rifle, driving the weapon into his chest, leaving him badly bruised. That made two narrow escapes from death. Harper wondered how many more chances he had left.

He moved around the immediate area, picking out the marks left by the horses, the footprints. He spotted the slender shape of Virginia's feet. He swore softly. Each time he was reminded of her the worry started again. He felt the swelling ache inside his skull again and touched the fingers of one hand to the crusted blood that had dried over the jagged wound. That last bullet had burned across his skull, just above his left ear. The wound had bled a lot, which was usual with superficial damage. What worried Harper more was the effect it might have on his already damaged memory. The long healing process going on inside his head might easily be set back by a further shock. It might even prevent the recovery he'd been hoping for. It was a cold and sobering thought, and not one on which to dwell. Concern over such a matter was something he could indulge himself in at a later time. He had more pressing involvements to handle first.

Harper took out his Colt, checking it thoroughly. Satisfied he put it away, searched around until he found his hat. He slapped the snow off it, buttoned his coat and moved off up the slope, stumbling through the deep snow. Even now his battered body was beginning to stiffen and he knew he was going to need to keep on the move. He followed the ragged line of tracks up through the boulder-strewn lower slopes and into the dark tree-line. Here he was forced to slow his pace. During daylight it was gloomy and shadowed beneath the trees. Now, with the approach of evening, it was fast becoming difficult to see the tracks at all. Harper persisted, his aching eyes seeking the winding trail of hoof prints. He was forced to backtrack more

80

than once when he lost the trail, wasting precious minutes locating his way again. He walked and fell and climbed to his feet and fell again. He moved like some dead creature which refused to lie down, determinedly dragging his aching, hurt body on through the tree-line until he broke out into the open further up the slopes. Harper paused for a moment, staring up the steep, endless slopes, and he cursed through cracked, frozen lips.

With the coming of the darkness a cold wind spun down off the high peaks. It cut through Harper's thick coat like a knife through butter, chilling him to the bone. He hunched his shoulders against the blast, his face bleak with the anger he was feeling for everything. It was an overpowering, raging sensation that suddenly exploded inside him, rising with a kind of self-generating power. It took control of him for a time and Harper stood motionless, helpless in its grip, a realization of what was causing his mood, but unable to do a damn thing about it. He lifted his face to the keen bite of the wind, letting it numb his flesh. He let the anger subside, let the pulse of rage settle itself. He felt calmer but still carried a mood of frustration, and he knew it wouldn't leave him until he'd learned what was going on. And the only way to find that out, he told himself, was to keep moving. To find out where Virginia was, what had happened to her, and why.

Despite his need for urgency Harper found a yearning for rest sweeping over him. His body had taken too much in the last hours. It begged for relief, for a chance to heal itself. Harper found he was slowing down. Every step was a battle which had to be won. He was almost rigid with cold. Fumbling his way around he eventually located a sloping bank with a shallow overhang at its base. Here he scraped away the snow until he'd exposed the hard ground beneath.

He built up the snow in a semi-circle around the front of the overhang, making himself a low wall which would protect him from the full force of the wind. Stumbling and slipping in the clinging, freezing snow Harper groped about in the darkness for fuel. He gathered what twigs and dead wood he could find, piling his find behind his wall of snow. When he figured he'd got enough he crouched down behind the wall and felt with stiff fingers for the box holding the few matches he had in one of his pockets, praying that they hadn't got wet.

He realized he needed something to start the fire with. Again he searched his pockets. All he found were a few crumpled dollar notes. A slow chuckle rose in his throat, forcing its way past his chattering teeth. Harper scraped one of the matches against a stone. It flared into life and went out before he had chance to touch it to one of the notes. He struck a second match, this time taking care to cup his hand around it as it burst into flame. He held the small yellow flame to the edge of one of the notes and watched the paper burn. Then he slipped it beneath the little pile of twigs he'd stacked up, feeding another note to help the first. The flames rose, smoke curling up from the damp wood. Harper watched the flame rise, then die down. He thrust in his last note. It caught, flared, flame rising. Then slowly the twigs began to burn, popping and hissing as moisture was boiled out of them. He watched his tiny fire grow and slowly fed it more fuel. It was a long, slow process, but gradually he increased the fuel until he was able to sit back and let it burn by itself. The orange-yellow flames threw out a comforting warmth and a soft circle of illumination. Beyond the ring of light lay what might have been eternal darkness. There was barely enough light to show where the trees ended and the sky began. Sitting before his tiny fire, accepting its meagre warmth, Harper looked about him, troubled, weary, not knowing what another day would bring. For one of the few times in his harsh and violent life he felt very lonely.

He always imagined he had become so used to the loneliness and isolation his work brought him, that nothing could crack the armour he had built around himself. He existed in a self-determining world of separation, where his days and often weeks slid by without much in the way of contact. Trailing some fugitive across endless miles of emptiness, surviving on his own instincts and his knowledge of the land, he might go for long periods where human contact didn't exist at all. He accepted that and the silence imposed on his waking hours had the effect of making him taciturn, less likely to speak even when he was in company. It had become the norm, but there were other times when he did engage in contact with others that the longing for human closeness wormed its way inside his protective shell and he craved that company. His time with Virginia had ignited that spark and now he was alone again he found he was missing her provocative banter.

Harper stared out beyond the ring of firelight, his mind alive with distorted images, and a knowledge that facts had popped unbidden into his conscious stream of thought.

Facts about his previous life. The loneliness and the lack of company. Where had that come from? Perhaps a slow remembrance of the missing parts of his life. They said something about him. About his life and his experiences. He refused to push the matter, realizing it would be safer to just allow them to return gradually.

Leaning forward he fed more wood onto the fire, making certain he avoided staring into the flames. Something instinctive told him not to do that. A sudden need to look into the darkness beyond and his vision would be affected by looking at the fire, taking precious seconds to adjust. In those seconds he could be dead.

Another trait from his past?

He hunched over, drawing as much of the fire's heat as he could and, as the warmth insinuated its way into his clothing, lulling him, slept. . . .

He awoke with a sudden start, his mind coming instantly alert, his sluggish body a second or so behind. Something told him, warned him, of an approaching danger. A presence which was close by. Harper fumbled his coat open, his right hand moving to the gun on his hip. His fingers gripped the butt hard, his thumb drawing back the hammer as he slid the gun free. He had pulled his body close against the low wall of snow jutting out from the overhang and he risked a quick glance over the top.

Nearby a handgun made a flat sound. Something clipped frozen snow from the top of the wall only an inch from Harper's face. Cold particles of hard snow peppered his face like icy buckshot. The stinging pain made him gasp. A second shot sounded and this bullet, lower, tore through the base of the wall, clipping the edge of Harper's left boot heel. Harper jerked his gun over the top of the wall, aiming quickly. He spotted the gunman now, catching a glimpse of powdersmoke from the second shot. A dark figure standing close to the knotted trunk of a towering tree, early-morning light glancing from the barrel of his gun as he made to fire again. Harper shot first. His bullet chewed a slice of bark from the tree. Wood chips exploded in the man's face. Harper heard him curse, saw him take a jerky step away from the tree's sheltering bulk. Harper steadied the Colt in both hands and triggered two more shots. Both caught the man in the chest, driving him back. He struck a tree just behind him and seemed to bounce off, falling face down in the snow. Harper stayed his ground, watching the man. There was no movement, but that didn't tell him anything. The man might still be alive, wounded maybe, but still capable of delivering a fatal shot from the gun which was still gripped in his outstretched hand.

Harper waited for almost half an hour. He wasn't in a fit enough condition to take risks. So he stayed where he was until he was damn sure the man was dead. Even when he climbed to his feet, unsteadily jerky-limbed after his long, cold night sleeping on the ground, he kept his Colt trained on the still figure. He'd taken time to reload while he'd been waiting and he was in the kind of mood where he would have pumped all six bullets into the man if he so much as quivered. By the time he'd reached him, standing over the body, Harper saw that he needn't have worried. The man was dead and had probably been that way from the moment he'd gone down. Both of Harper's bullets had gone through his heart, blasting out between his shoulders. The snow beneath the body was stained a deep pink. Harper rolled the body over, staring down into the face of the man who had just tried to kill him. Something stirred in the tangled depths of Harper's mind as he looked into the face of the dead man. There was some-thing very familiar about the features. The dark skin, black eyes, the broad, heavy-boned face. The tangled hair was black too. His name?

His name? Harper struggled to draw it from his memory.

It came by itself. As if it had been waiting for his summons.

Puma.

That was his name. A half-breed killer. A gun for hire who would kill anyone, anywhere, any way. In a rush now the images came flooding back.

Puma.

A man Harper had almost tangled with once before.

There it was again. Another faint sliver of information that told him of his previous association with the man he had just killed. No hard detail. Just a shadowy recall that confirmed he *did* know Puma. There had been a close confrontation, he remembered, but something had happened to break it up. Somewhere down in the flat-lands. A cattle dispute. He couldn't recall any more. It was unimportant now. What did matter was the fact that he had remembered *something* more from his past. A face and a name. If it could happen once it could happen again.

Harper walked away from Puma's body. If Puma had come looking for him it implied he was in with the people who had taken Virginia. It also told Harper that there was a horse nearby. He had only been retracing Puma's foot-prints for a couple of minutes when he came on the horse tethered to the low branch of a tree. Harper checked the animal thoroughly. It was a strong, powerfully built animal, the kind needed for riding through conditions which existed on these mountain slopes. A Henry .44-40 rifle lay in the saddle sheath, a filled canteen hung from the saddle horn. In a sack behind the saddle Harper found ammunition, food and cooking gear. There was coffee, too, and a half bottle of whiskey. Even a bundle of cheap cigars. A crumpled box of matches wrapped in a scrap of oilcloth.

He took the horse back to his resting place and tethered it. He built up his fire, which had almost gone out, and when the flames were high he put on a pot of coffee. From the supplies on Puma's horse, Harper fried thick slices of salted bacon. He was ravenous but he forced himself to eat slowly. Too much food in an empty stomach could leave him a damn sight worse off than before he had eaten.

He could see the body of the man named Puma from where he was sitting. A chill that had nothing to do with the weather ran through him when he realized how close he'd come to dying. It could have been over before he'd been able to register what was happening. Yet something had brought him out of sleep, warning him, giving him the chance to defend himself. He couldn't put his finger on what it might be. Only some kind of instinctive capacity for survival. Whatever it was he had reason to be thankful for it.

He finished the food and downed as much of the hot coffee as he could. Then he packed away the gear, checked the horse and the rifle Puma had carried, climbed into the saddle and moved off.

He picked up the trail Puma had made on the way in and followed it back through the trees, finally breaking out on the edge of a flat meadow. He rode across the meadow, skirting the rim of a small, narrow lake, its frozen surface streaked with powdered snow. A pale sun threw warmth across the land. It brightened the day but did little to reduce the low temperature. The air tasted fresh and sharp. It was crystal clear, letting him see for miles across the white landscape. Harper estimated that Bannock couldn't be more than a day's ride away. But had Virginia's captors taken her direct to the town? The trail he was following still led him north, but there was plenty of time for it to change direction. All he could do was to stay with it and hope that they wouldn't be expecting him.

He rode at a steady pace, not wanting to push the horse beneath him. The way ahead had the appearance of being safe, but he knew that layers of snow might easily hide traps for the unwary. Holes, sudden drop-offs, even deep gullies, could lie just below the surface. A simple mistake could cripple his horse, putting the animal through pain and suffering and, at worse, leaving him set afoot. He had no intention of that happening. Virginia's survival could be depending on him finding her before something drastic took place. He had taken the job of escorting her through the mountains, placing her under his protection. He had no intention of reneging on that promise. As much for himself as for Virginia.

10

It was midday when they came in sight of the abandoned way-station. It had been years since the stage line had gone out of business, mainly due to the coming of the railroad, but in part due to the fact that the man who had set up the route hadn't taken into consideration the difficulties of taking six-horse Concords up and down such mountainous terrain. Other stage lines, taking more care over their routes, had prospered, while the dispirited owner of this particular venture, seeing the error of his ways and his falling bank balance, took a train back East. The stock was sold off, the employees moved on, and the way-stations were left to rot.

The only sign of life Virginia could see was a pale plume of smoke rising from the stone chimney at one end of the low timber building. The fact they seemed to have arrived at their destination did little to upset her.

She had already experienced enough terror over the last couple of days to numb her for months to come. Whatever lay in store for her inside that building, it made no impression on her. She watched Jed Cooper slip from his saddle before the building and reach out to take the reins of her own horse.

'Get down,' Cole Shannuck's voice snapped. He was off his own horse, standing beside hers, prodding her thigh with a hard finger. 'You hear me? Move it, lady.'

Virginia dismounted, pushing back the anger which boiled up inside her. She faced Shannuck squarely. 'Shannuck, you are a loud-mouthed bully!'

Shannuck gave a tight-lipped grin, and then slapped her across the face. The force of the blow pushed Virginia back, only the bulk of her horse stopping her from falling to the ground. She touched a hand to the burning spot on her cheeks, refusing to lower her angered gaze from Shannuck's face.

'Thank you for proving what I just said,' she told him.

Shannuck muttered something obscene, grabbed her arms and dragged her towards the building. Reaching the door he booted it open, hauling Virginia into the dimly lit room. He didn't stop there but simply propelled Virginia across the floor. Struggling against his brutal grip Virginia caught sight of dark-clad figures on the far side of the room. She counted four of them, bunched around a fire blazing in an open hearth, bulky in their thick coats. She had little time to see anything else. Shannuck pushed open another door and shoved her into a dark room. Before he closed and bolted the door Virginia made out the shape of a low bunk against one wall. There was only one window in the room and she saw the thick planks which had been nailed across it, blocking it off. Then the door banged shut and she was left alone in the semi-darkness. Alone, wondering, cold, and, she admitted, a little frightened suddenly.

Turning from the door he'd just bolted, Shannuck strode

across the room, working open his heavy coat. He tossed it aside as he reached the group of men around the fire. Shannuck eased his way through to the welcome swell of heat and stood while the chill was thawed from his bones.

'I was beginning to think you weren't going to make it!'

The speaker was a tall, fair-haired man in his thirties. Starting to run to fat in his face. Might have been good-looking a few years back but he had let himself go. His name was Jerome Cortland and he was the man calling the shots on this deal. The man with the money.

Shannuck glanced at the speaker. He did not like Jerome Cortland very much. *No*, he corrected, *not at all.* But the man was paying well and for enough money Cole Shannuck could put up with anybody.

'More problems, Shannuck?' Cortland asked.

Shannuck smiled tiredly. 'Many as you need,' he said.

'Just tell it, Shannuck. I can do without the jokes,' Cortland snapped.

'Benteen started it. I sent him down into Butte to keep an eye on the woman. Trouble was she'd already gone and hired herself some help. Man named Harper. Done some star packing and worked for bounty. Good man with a gun. Benteen must have braced him. Way I see it Harper must have killed him. By the time we found this out the woman and Harper had moved out. They were heading for Bannock. When we caught up with 'em Harper put up one hell of a fight. Feeney and Cleaver are both dead. I reckon me and Cooper would have been if I hadn't gotten some lead into that bastard. Harper always was a tough son of a bitch.'

'*Jesus!*' The exclamation came from one of the other men. He turned to glare at Cortland. 'This whole thing is

91

turning into a massacre. What next, Jerry? Will it be our turn?'

Cortland gave a nervous chuckle. 'I don't think we'll be having any more trouble from this man Harper.' He glanced at Shannuck. 'Will we, Cole?'

'I put him down myself. He went into a gully. If the bullet didn't kill him the cold would have finished him. Way back we run into Puma and I sent him to make sure Harper was dead. Told him where to find the others and to bury 'em all. We come across Jack Bell too. He was dead.'

The man who had brought himself into the conversation pointed a thin finger at Cortland. 'Hell, Jerry, we'd better be damn sure there ain't any loose ends left lying around.'

'I think all the loose ends have been tidied up, Ben,' Cortland said. 'Once Puma has buried the bodies we won't need to worry. He'll place them where they'll never be found. It's unfortunate that these problems have developed but I see no reason why we can't just carry on.'

Ben Holland grunted. He still wasn't fully convinced. There was too much at stake to be as casual as Cortland. There was a lot to be said for the cautious approach. It was the way Holland had always operated and he didn't see any reason for changing his ways now. Not even for the amount of money involved in Cortland's grandiose scheme. He had been talked into the deal because whatever else Cortland had a persuasive tongue and he excelled at setting deals. Holland, who was known in the territory, had the muscle and the contacts to run with the deal.

'No matter how many millions you're figurin' on, Jerry,

if we get caught it ain't going to do any of us much good if we're in jail. Or on the end of a rope.'

Shannuck chuckled softly. 'For a gambling man, Holland, you sure are the nervous kind. How the hell did you ever get where you are?

'By knowing just when to put up and when to hold off,' Holland said. 'And by hiring dummies like you to do the dirty work for me.'

A hard growl of anger rose in Shannuck's throat. He moved towards Holland but paused when the remaining two men flanking Holland, also moved.

For a moment tension held them in a potentially dangerous situation. It was Cortland who broke it up.

'Cole, cut it out. Look, men, it isn't going to make things any better if we argue amongst ourselves. Let's just calm down and talk this out. There's too much to lose.'

Cole Shannuck relaxed visibly, his broad shoulders dropping. He turned away from the fire. At that moment the outer door opened and Jed Cooper stepped inside. He closed the door and stood for a moment to shake snow from his coat.

'Damn storm's building up again,' he announced, and when there was no reply he glanced towards the tight group of men gathered before the fire. Cooper stared from face to face, quick to catch the angry expressions. 'I miss something?' he asked, crossing the room.

Cortland was the first to react. 'Just a slight misunderstanding, Jed. Nothing to get worried over.'

'Glad to hear it,' Cooper said. He eyed his partner for a long moment. 'Cole?'

Shannuck rubbed at his unshaven jaw with a fierce flick of his hand. 'Nothing to bother over,' he said. 'Let's go and see if there's any coffee on in the kitchen.'

'Sure,' Cooper agreed. He followed Shannuck's towering figure, unease etched across his face.

'Christ, Ben, take it easy,' Cortland said, when Shannuck and Cooper were out of earshot. 'Cole might be no more than a gunman but don't forget he's one of the best. He's hard and he's proud.'

Ben Holland dismissed his two bodyguards. The two men faded out of sight in a dark corner of the room. Holland and Cortland pulled up a couple of hard chairs in front of the fire and sat down.

'Regardless of everything else,' Cortland said, 'we've got her here. That was what we set out to do.' A triumphant smile washed across his round, slightly puffy face. 'She's in that room over there, Ben, and she's our way to millions. Cash, shares, bonds. Property, mines, timber. Hell, there's a list as long as my arm. And right now it's as good as ours. Ours, Ben. The whole damn lot.'

Holland nodded. 'Yeah? Well, tell me all that again when we've got it lying on a table in front of us.'

'With Virginia out of the way there's no problem.' Cortland sat back, allowing himself a satisfied smirk. 'For God's sake, Ben, relax. Our troubles are over!'

11

The weather changed again dramatically. The first indication was a sudden darkening in the sky. Then the sun vanished behind heavy, dense clouds that came rolling in from over the bleak crests of the mountain peaks. Shadows lengthened, it became colder, and within a relatively short time the landscape was altered.

The storm caught Sam Harper out in the open. He was moving slowly across the face of a long slope when the wind drove down from the lead grey sky. Thick flakes of snow danced around him, swiftly building to a heavy fall. Within minutes Harper was lost in a white fog of swirling, blinding snow. He drew his coat in around his body, jamming his sodden hat tight down over his face and swore in vain at the contrary elements. The tracks he'd been following vanished before his eyes, hidden by the fresh fall of snow. All Harper could do was to take a guess at the direction they might take. He was certain of one thing: Bannock was not their destination. Virginia's captors had cut away from the town miles back. They had started to curve off towards the west.

But to where?

Somewhere at the back of Harper's mind existed a very

faint image of the map Virginia had produced, the one Jack Bell had sent her, on which she had marked her own route to Bannock. Somewhere on that map he had seen a location, below and to the west of Bannock. Harper couldn't recall what it had been but it stuck in his mind now, an irritating thorn that kept nagging at him as he rode.

The need to find her safe and well burned hard inside him. A responsibility that refused to diminish. He thought about the way he was feeling and unbidden, the knowledge showed itself. This was another part of his make-up. A steadfast determination not to fail someone for whom he had accepted responsibility. It was in his character. A desire not to let them down. It wasn't a forced decision. It just existed. He thought about that and wondered what it was that made it so important to him. Perhaps, he decided, there had been something in his past that had left a deep imprint in his mind that made him incapable of betraying someone's trust. Whatever it might be, it held him to the unspoken promise.

Don't give in, Virginia. Hang on. I won't quit on you.

The wind became stronger hurling the white eddies of snow down from the high peaks. Harper felt the stuff clinging to his clothing, forming a wet blanket over his horse's flanks. He was beginning to feel cold again. No amount of thick clothing was going to keep out the cold during a storm of such ferocity. Harper blinked the thick flakes away from his eyes, pawing them from his cold face.

His horse began to play awkward. The animal didn't take to the inclement weather. Harper could see its point but he had no choice.

There was no time for sheltering from the weather. Bad

or not he had to keep moving. Harper yanked savagely on the reins, digging in his heels. The horse lunged forward, floundering in deep snow. It fought against Harper's heavy hand but it couldn't win. Reluctantly it plodded on, head down, hating the weather and the rider on its back.

Harper kept reviewing the image in his mind of the map. Something on it had lodged in his mind.

What was it?

He struggled to bring the details into his mind's eye. His struggle to stay alert; the numbing cold of the driving storm; all these factors held him back from clear thinking. He felt sure the location was important. But what was it? Where was it? Close, or far away? Had he passed it without knowing? He had done his best to keep his line of travel constant, but the vagaries of pinpointing landmarks in the middle of the storm meant he could have ridden by and was now travelling along a different path.

No!

He refused to let that be true. He had maintained his route. Of that he was sure. Harper reined in, easing in the saddle as he took a long, slow look around, checking his position. He scanned the dark, brooding peaks looming overhead. The silent mountains held many secrets and were reluctant to give them away. Harper checked his back trail. The drifting snow had already covered his tracks. He sat his horse in a white wasteland of smooth, unmarked snow, a lone figure made small in the vast expanse of the mountain slopes. The only sound he could hear was the soft moan of the wind as it shivered its way down off the higher peaks, pushing the snow before it, swirling it and dropping it around him as if it was deliberately attempting to conceal the way ahead.

Harper sat upright, a tight smile edging his chapped lips.

That was it!

The way ahead! The missing detail.

A way-station!

Abandoned when the stage line went bust! That was it. The recall jolted Harper out of his lethargy. That was what he'd seen on Virginia's map. Just the place to take someone if the intention was to keep that person hidden away. It seemed a likely destination for Virginia and her captors. And in this weather a safe haven between Butte and Bannock. There was no guarantee that was where they had gone but Harper figured the odds were high enough to justify a visit. He was starting to have a feeling there was hope after all. All he had to do now was to find the damn place.

Despite the fury of the storm Harper was able to keep a check on his line of travel by the ever-present mountain peaks. He used them as markers, keeping them in the same position as he rode. He stopped every so often to make sure he hadn't drifted off course. Even so he began to despair of ever sighting the way-station. He might pass it and not even notice the place in this storm. Drifting snow could rise to surprising heights, especially up here in this bleak mountain country.

He rode on, driven by a compulsive need to stay unbeaten. There was something deep inside which kept him going, not allowing him the luxury of even thinking about giving in. It was not in Harper's make-up, that much he did know about himself. He might do a lot of things and probably had, but he was damned certain that quitting because the game got too hard was not one of them. He had also made a deal with Virginia Maitland: a promise to see her safely to her destination, and he wasn't about to go back on his word.

And in the end his dogged persistence paid off.

The howling wind was driving down out of an ever darkening sky when his aching eyes picked out the faint, dark shape of a long, low building, half-hidden by rolling drifts of snow. Harper eased his horse into the scant shelter of some tall pines. He dismounted, tied the horse, and took the rifle he'd acquired from Puma with him, checking it again to make sure it was fully loaded and cocked. He moved silently down through the pines until he was close enough to the building to be able to make out the glow of lamplight shining through dirty windows. At the rear of the building there was a corral and a narrow lean-to. Harper could make out the dark bulk of a number of horses stirring restlessly beneath the lean-to.

He hunched down with his back to one of the pine trunks. Fishing around in his pocket he brought out one of the cigars he'd found in Puma's saddle-bags. He lit it. Smoking the cigar slowly, his nose wrinkling against the acrid taste of the cheap, bitter tobacco, Harper studied the layout of the way-station. If they had Virginia in there how the hell was he going to get her out? He had no way of knowing how many were in there with her. Just the two who had brought her? Or had others been waiting for them? Harper flicked dead ash from the tip of the cigar and realized that it had gone out. He crushed it in his fingers and tossed it aside. He could sit out here until he froze to the ground and he still wouldn't know any more. The only way he was going to find answers to his questions was by going down there and taking Virginia away from whoever was holding her. And the hell with anyone who got in his way. He was mad enough to kill on sight! Of late he'd been knocked about and shot at and been half frozen – and the maddening thing was he still didn't know why. Virginia's visit to Montana seemed to have sparked off an awful lot of violence for some odd reason. Sam Harper had already reached the point where he was tired of being on the receiving end. From here on in he was going to hand out the trouble to anyone who stood in his way. He checked his handgun. Something told him he was going to need his weapons.

Slipping from the shelter of the trees Harper cut quickly across the open ground, keeping his eyes on the door of the building. He reached the comparative safety of the end wall without difficulty and paused there to catch his breath. Moving along the base of the end wall he made for the rear of the building. As he had been approaching the place, he had thought about the horses under the lean-to. It shouldn't take but a minute to slip their tethers and set them loose, he decided. At the rear he stopped and spent a couple of minutes making certain they didn't have a man on guard. He saw nothing, heard nothing. Finally he eased his way along the rear of the building, slipping beneath the lean-to. His cold fingers fumbled with the knots of the tethers but eventually he had them loose. Harper shooed the horses out into the open. They didn't think a great deal of the idea and kept crowding back towards the lean-to. Harper cursed them foully, but silently, hating the stubborn cussedness of the animals. After a couple of minutes he was sweating freely beneath his thick clothing, and not all of it was from exer-

100

tion. The horses, tiring of his persistent attempts to drive them away, suddenly turned and ploughed off through the thick snow. Almost immediately they were lost from view by the falling snow.

While he had been dealing with the horses, Harper had noticed the door at the rear of the building. It most probably led to the kitchen. He moved to it and peered in through the small window set in the wall adjacent to the door. He'd been right. He could make out the shadowed outlines of kitchen equipment. Turning his attention to the door he tried it and found it unlocked. Easing the door open Harper slipped inside and pressed himself against the watt. There was a fire burning in the cook stove, throwing pleasant warmth out across the room. A pot of coffee simmered gently. The rich aroma reached Harper and made his stomach growl. He had to pull himself away from the stove. It didn't matter how he felt, now wasn't the time to be filling his empty stomach.

He was in the act of reaching for the handle of the door leading through to the main part of the building when it swung open and a man stepped into the kitchen. The man was coatless and had a coffee cup in his hand. Harper recognized him as one of the riders who had chased Harper and Virginia across the mountain slopes. Before the man could react, Harper jammed the muzzle of his rifle into his throat.

'Close the door,' Harper told him quietly. 'Now move away from it.'

Harper took the man's handgun and placed it on the kitchen table.

He could feel the man's eyes on him and realized that he probably looked a mess. Frozen snow caked his clothes

101

and was plastered over his face. Dark hair hanging from beneath his hat was crusted with blood from the wound in his scalp.

'I ain't dead, friend,' Harper said harshly, 'but you're likely to be if I don't get the answers I want.'

Jed Cooper stayed silent. The hard muzzle of the rifle was boring a painful hole in his throat. He had no intention of doing anything liable to cause Sam Harper to react violently. He had already witnessed Harper's skill with a gun. He needed no convincing.

'How many more of you are there out there?'

'Five out there and me.' Cooper was surprised at the way his voice emerged as a dry croak.

'Where's the woman?' Harper emphasized his second question with a savage thrust of the gun barrel.

'*All right*! All right! Just take it easy, Harper, the woman's not been hurt. She's in one of the back rooms.'

Harper nodded. He removed the barrel of the rifle from Cooper's throat. The gunman relaxed. Then he caught the cold gleam in Sam Harper's eyes and realized he wasn't off the hook. His realization came too late. The rifle barrel slashed down with brutal efficiency across Cooper's skull. Cooper uttered a short grunt of pain as he went down.

The door opened silently. Harper studied the layout of the big room before him. What little furniture there was had been grouped close to the fire blazing in the open hearth. A couple of dusty lamps cast a subdued light across the bare floor. Harper's attention was caught by the men around the fire. The man in the kitchen hadn't been lying. Including him there *were* six. There was only one face Harper knew amongst the five warming themselves by the fire. The big man who had led the chase out on the mountain. Somewhere on the fringes of his mind lurked a name for the man. Harper didn't force the matter. It would come of its own volition, as had Puma's name.

Putting his back to the wall, Harper edged across the floor until he was in a position that enabled him to cover the five men beside the fire. Drawing back the hammer on the rifle he said, 'Don't anybody do a damn thing liable to make me pull this trigger. Just turn round and keep your hands in sight.'

Heads turned in his direction. Eyes noted the levelled rifle, the hard face above it, and decided to be advised of Harper's warning. All except one. A sallow-faced man dressed in a dark suit. He was one of Holland's body-guards. Tall and thin, with the complexion of someone used to existing indoors, the man simply stepped off to one side, his slim white hand darting to the heavy gun he wore strapped to his chest beneath his coat. It was a fool-ish move, but like many in his trade the man had a repu-tation to back up. There was also that tinge of imagined invulnerability that some of these fast guns carried with them. Like this one, they were usually mistaken about their own proficiency – or lack of it.

Harper seemed barely to move. But the rifle flickered across to line up with the thin man. The rifle cracked harshly, powdersmoke adding its stench to the musky air. The thin gunman whirled backwards, blood spurting from a hole in his chest. His heels caught in the base of the hearth and his body fell back into the flames of the fire. He began to scream as the flames blistered the flesh of his face and hands. A sickly smell filled the room. Before the others could do anything the gunman flopped forward out of the fire. He slid awkwardly across the floor, his body kicking feebly. Smoke curled lazily up from the smouldering cloth of his suit.

'Anybody want to join him?' Harper asked. 'Now if any of you are carrying guns I want them on the floor. Out where I can see them. And make it fast!'

They did what they were told, conscious of the dead man at their feet.

'I'll get you before you leave this mountain, Harper,' Cole Shannuck said.

Harper grinned savagely. 'You tried once and I'm still here. So did that Indian – the one they called Puma, and he won't be hiring out again.'

'You killed him?' Shannuck asked.

Harper nodded. 'He was begging for it.'

One of the men, standing next to Shannuck, said, 'Damnit, Cole, you told me he was dead.'

Shannuck shrugged. 'Looks like I was wrong, Cortland.' He grinned abruptly, showing large teeth. 'You want me to do something about it?'

'Now look. . . .'

'Shut it, mister,' Harper said. 'I don't care a damn how you sort out your problems. You can do it after I leave. You,' he said, pointing at Ben Holland, 'go and bring the woman out here. Do one thing that doesn't look right to me and I'll shoot your head right off your shoulders.'

Holland moved quickly across the floor. He worked the bolt on one of the doors leading off from the main room and shoved it open.

'Virginia, you in there?' Harper called.

After a moment her voice reached him. 'Is that you, Sam?'

104

'Yeah. Now get out here quick.'

She emerged from the room stepping by the scowling figure of Ben Holland.

'I thought you were dead. I was sure they'd killed you.'

'They tried.'

Virginia stared at him. 'You took terrible. Are you all right?'

'Don't worry about me. Just pick up those guns and toss 'em out of the nearest window. Might be a notion to keep one for yourself.'

She did as he suggested. With something close to reluctance she retained one of the guns. As she moved back to join Harper her eyes drifted over the faces of the men before the fire and a shocked gasp rose in her throat, 'Oh no, Jerome, not you!'

'Somebody you know?' Harper asked.

Virginia did not answer. She simply stood and stared into the face of Jerome Cortland, unable to take in what had been revealed to her.

'*Virginia?*' Harper asked again. 'We ain't got all day to stand around. Just tell me what's going on.'

'I think I'm beginning to understand a lot of things now,' Virginia said. 'You see, Sam, this man here is Jerome Cortland. He is a lawyer. His father's firm has handled Maitland business for years. Just over a year ago Hendly Cortland died and Jerome took control of the practice. My father was never happy with his handling of our business. He didn't like Jerome's methods. It seems he might not have been a bad judge. Or am I wrong, Jerome?'

Jerome Cortland allowed himself a thin smile. 'As astute as ever, dear Virginia. Unfortunately this time your awareness of the situation will do you no good. The fact that you have stumbled upon my involvement in this little affair will not detract from the purpose of you having been drawn to this place. That being your untimely and tragic death.'

'Then I *was* right!' Virginia said. 'All those problems the mines have been having. They were created with the sole intention of bringing me out here. That's why Jack Bell was murdered. He knew too much and he would have spoiled your plans.'

'You see,' Cortland said. 'I told you she was clever. Too damn clever for a woman.'

'And too rich for your liking?' Harper asked. 'Is that what it comes down to, Cortland? The fact that she has all that money? All that power? Sticks in your craw?'

Jerome Cortland's face darkened with seething anger. 'Hell, yes! When her old man died it all fell in her lap. Millions. Every damned asset belonging to Maitland. I know just how much. We've been handling Maitland business for years. Contracts. Stocks. Property deals. Cash transfers. It's all been through our hands.'

'You sound as if you hate me for it, Jerome,' Virginia said.

Cortland scowled at her. 'I do. You had it all. So easily. All I had was a small-time law practice with no chance of expansion. My father might have been a lawyer but he was no businessman. The firm was in debt and so was I. So I began to siphon off money from the Maitland account. It was simple at first and I could cover myself easily. Selling off a few shares here and there. The trouble was a little didn't cover my needs. So I began to work on a scheme that would let me get my hands on a larger share.'

'The thefts at the mines? The violence? It was all your

doing?' Virginia's face darkened with a sudden anger. 'Were you trying to force down the price of Maitland shares so you could buy cheaply?'

'It worked. A few discreet words here and there about Maitland Copper being in trouble. Some physical assistance from my friends here.' Cortland grinned. 'Shareholders are fickle creatures. Just a smell of trouble and they can't unload their stock fast enough.'

Harper said, 'My guess is that you weren't satisfied with that. You wanted Virginia out of the way. Dead in fact.'

'People have been killed for a lot less,' Cortland snapped. His tone indicated that he thought his explanation justified what he had done.

'How would my death work for you?' Virginia asked.

'The legal complexities involved with such an empire as yours are endless. There are still various aspects of your father's estate to be sorted out. If you were to suddenly die, leaving the Maitland businesses in a sort of legal limbo, it could be years before things could be settled. As the appointed executor of Maitland business it would be easy for me to manipulate and control share dealing, cash flow. You may remember, Virginia, that there was a condition in your father's will which stipulated that in the event of you not being able to keep control of the businesses, the Cortland law firm would step in and assume full responsibility until such time as a new manager was appointed, or someone bought the controlling interest. Your father, Virginia, had great faith in my father. He was not as happy with my way of doing things. If he had lived longer I think he might have changed the conditions of his will. Fortunately for me he died before he could, and that left me in an extremely powerful position providing you could be removed from the scene.'

'I must give you credit for your plans, Jerome. It took a keen mind to work out a scheme like yours. Twisted, but keen.'

'And all for nothing,' Harper put in drily.

Jerome Cortland shrugged. 'Maybe. Thing is you aren't in the clear yet.'

'You forgetting who has the gun?' Harper asked.

'Having it and using it are two different matters,' Cortland said. 'You intend to shoot us all, Harper?'

'Ask him,' Harper suggested, indicated Shannuck.

Cole Shannuck smiled grimly. 'I was you, Cortland, I wouldn't push it too far.'

'He won't do it,' Cortland said. 'Am I right, Virginia?'

'Killing in cold blood seems to be your style, Jerome. Not mine,' Virginia replied. 'Sam, take me away from here. Now.'

Harper looked from Shannuck's grinning face to Virginia. There wasn't a thing he could do. No matter how he felt about these men he wasn't going to kill them where they stood. Leaving them alive meant that they would eventually follow. There would not be any hesitation on their part if it came to another confrontation. If Harper and Virginia reached the nearest lawman and told their story, Cortland and his cronies were finished. They would do their damnedest to try and stop that from happening. He wished he was in a position to take them along, under his gun, and deliver them personally into the hands of the law. But that was impossible. He and Virginia were going to have their hands full trying to get away themselves. Dragging along five hostile and violent men in the conditions outside was beyond Harper. He didn't even contemplate it.

'Let's go,' he said to Virginia.

As they moved towards the door, Cole Shannuck said, 'You'll never make it, Harper. Wherever you go, we'll be following you. Next time we meet I'll have a gun in my hand.'

Sam Harper paused at the door. 'I were you I'd head for the Canadian border. First time I see one of your faces I'll start shooting. And that's a promise I'll keep!'

He stepped outside, dragging the door shut. Thick snow swirled around him instantly. Harper grabbed Virginia's arm and led her away from the station, up towards the place where he'd left his horse. Only now did he curse his stupidity at not keeping back one of the horses he'd so easily run off. Now he and Virginia were going to have to ride double.

Damn fool, he thought. *The cold's affecting your thinking!*

As they reached the trees, slipping and sliding in the thick snow, Harper heard the flat sound of a handgun. The bullet whacked into the ground yards away. Harper shoved Virginia in front. More shots followed but they were all wide. Somebody was letting his feelings mar his aim.

'Over there,' he said, spotting his tethered horse. He yanked the reins loose and swung up into the saddle. Leaning over he took hold of Virginia's arm and yanked her up behind him.

'For God's sake hold on tight!' he yelled.

'You don't have to tell me,' she yelled back.

Harper jerked the horse's head around and put it up the slope beyond the trees. As they broke out of the timber a rifle opened up and wood splinters exploded in his face. Bullets caromed from the trunks, showering them with bark splinters. Harper heard Virginia gasp once but her arms retained their rigid grasp around his waist. Harper yelled and swore at the horse, driving it on up the steep slope. As they crested the ridge and lost sight of the way-station he breathed a sigh of relief. They weren't out of trouble yet but at least they might have a short respite. There would not be any pursuit until the men back at the station had recovered their horses. The longer it took them the better became Harper's chance of gaining some distance.

He drew rein long enough to get his bearings, turning the horse towards Bannock. The mine town was closest. If he and Virginia could get there before Cortland and his bunch then they stood a chance.

'What's the law like in Bannock?' he asked over his shoulder.

'Honest as far as I know,' Virginia said. 'Right now, though, I'm not sure I'd trust the President himself.'

Harper made no reply. He realized that Virginia had just experienced a shattering revelation. Not only had she exposed the man responsible for her business difficulties, she had also learned that the same man, supposedly work-ing for her best interests, had engineered the attempts on her life.

'They really do mean it when they say they'll kill us,' Virginia said, after a couple of minutes.

'They have to,' Harper replied. 'As long as we're alive we can tell our story. Once that happens they're finished. But if they can stop us before we reach Bannock they could still pull the whole thing off.'

'It was madness leaving them alive. We've just set ourselves up as targets. Haven't we?'

'Yeah. I'm not arguing over that.'

'We couldn't have done anything else, could we? It's the difference between them and us. They would have killed us without a second thought. Does that make *us* stupid?'

'No. It makes us human. Hell, I'm no damn saint, Virginia. I've killed, but only because it was forced on me through circumstances. If the truth was known maybe I've done some damn mean things too, but the way that bunch goes about it makes my flesh creep.'

'All for money. Just because I have money and they don't. But why should I feel guilty about it? My father made his money honestly. Now it's mine. Selfish or not, Sam Harper, I don't intend letting someone like Jerome Cortland get his hands on it.'

'I believe you. Anyhow I got to get you to Bannock alive for a very good reason.'

'Oh? What's that?'

'You haven't paid me yet.'

There was a brief silence behind him. And then Virginia Maitland began to laugh. The sound rose above them, clear and light. It was the most pleasant sound Harper had heard for a long time. He hoped he lived long enough to be able to hear it again.

12

Harper knew they weren't going to make Bannock that day. The darkness slid in around them like a black fog. The falling snow added to the confusion. Before the light failed completely, he scouted round for somewhere they could stay the night. The best he came up with was a low overhang at the base of a high rock face. A tangled mass of snow-coated thick brush concealed it from prying eyes. Harper dismounted and led the horse to the overhang. He tethered the animal close by.

'Come on,' he said to Virginia.

She peered down at him. Weariness had caught up with her and she was practically asleep in the saddle. Harper reached up and pulled her off the horse. Her legs gave as she touched the ground and she lay against Harper, too tired to move.

'Give me a minute,' Harper said. He left her and moved to the horse. Freeing the bedroll from behind the saddle he opened it up. There were a couple of blankets and an oilskin slicker. Harper bent beneath the overhang and laid the slicker on the cold ground, then spread one of the blankets.

'That looks marvellous,' he heard Virginia say.

112

When he had her settled on the blanket Harper covered her with the second one. Leaving her he went to the horse and returned with food, water and cooking utensils. He foraged around for wood. Carefully shredding a few twigs he struck a match and held his breath until the wood caught. Patiently he added to the tiny flicker, letting it build slowly. He knew that what he was doing was wrong. A fire was one way of attracting attention but both he and Virginia needed hot food and drink inside them. It was a risk he was prepared to take. Once he had the fire burning brightly Harper sliced up the remaining bacon and dropped it into the pan. He prepared hot water and dropped in some crushed coffee beans. As the smell of frying bacon and hot coffee reached his nostrils his stomach began to growl. Even Virginia roused herself from the half-sleep that had swept over her. She lifted her head and watched Harper's preparations.

'I never thought food could smell so good,' she said.

Harper poured scalding coffee into the tin mug. Before he handed it to her he added a measure of whiskey from the bottle he'd found in Puma's gear. Virginia took it and sniffed the mug.

'What have you put in it?' she inquired.

'Just a drop of something to warm you up.'

Virginia took a swallow. Her face screwed up in mock agony for a moment. 'My God, Sam, what are you trying to do? Get me drunk?'

'Tough tycoon like you? I figure you can take it.'

Between them they cleared the fried bacon from the pan and emptied the pot of coffee. As soon as the meal was over Harper extinguished the fire and cleared away the remains. He took his rifle and sat with his back to the

113

rear of the overhang.

'Do you think they'll find us in the dark?'

'They'd be foolish to try until morning. Blundering around in the dark is liable to get them lost, or get them falling down a crevasse. Way Cole Shannuck works he'll get them to stay put until dawn, then set off after us.'

'Let's hope he sees it like that then.'

'Try and get some sleep,' he told Virginia. 'Soon as it's light we'll move out.'

Virginia propped herself up on her elbows. 'Are you planning to sit there all night?'

'Yeah.'

'That's ridiculous!' Virginia sat up. 'You could freeze. Now stop acting like I was a nun and come over here.'

Harper joined her beneath the blanket. He felt the pressure of her supple body against his as she settled herself. Virginia turned her face towards him, a soft blur in the near blackness.

'British reserve isn't all it's made out to be,' she said softly. 'Goodnight, Sam.'

'Miss Maitland,' he replied with mock civility.

Harper lay for a long time, staring out beyond the overhang. Through the snowfall all he could see was pitch black. Almost too dark to believe there was anything beyond their own place. Yet he knew there was nothing unreal about their situation. It was still dangerous and would stay that way until they managed to reach Bannock. Maybe even then things might not change dramatically. Harper had long ago ceased to believe in happy endings. Matters had a way of working themselves out eventually – but never in a neat and tidy way. There were always complications.

114

Beside him the sleeping woman stirred. Her closeness and her warmth lulled his senses. He felt sleep approaching. Virginia twisted on to her side, one arm sliding across Harper's chest. She drew herself closer to him, seeking the security of his body, and he was made acutely aware of her unassuming sensuality. It would have been an easy thing to allow himself to be attracted by her. She was a beautiful young woman. Desirable. The need was there on his part and the temptation to succumb. Yet he hesitated. Had he allowed such things to happen before? And had he suffered for it? Maybe other people had been hurt. He sat up suddenly, staring wildly out into the darkness as a powerful surge of strong memories came flooding back, unchecked. A tangled torrent of faces and names and of places and happenings that overwhelmed him. He was powerless to prevent them erupting into his conscious mind. His family. His father a disappointed man who struggled to keep the small ranch going against the odds. Harsh weather, disease, a drop in the price of beef. The thieving that had brought the final blow, turning his father into a shambling figure, his dreams shattered. And his mother, once pretty, aged before her time. Lined and grey-haired, taking any menial job until her health gave out and she died before her fortieth year. He and his father had buried her in the windswept landscape and the day after his father had ridden out without a backward look. It was the last time he ever saw the man.

At 16 he was abandoned. It made him a survivor and over the next few years he worked for anyone who would employ him. All he knew then was the cattle business so he signed on with drives heading for the railheads. It gave him experience, taught him hard lessons and by the time he was in his early twenties he had the respect of those he rode with. Part was down to his skill as a drover, but more respect came from his natural ability with the gun he carried on his hip. He had never once thought about it as anything but a tool, until the day he found himself in an argument with a loud-mouthed drover from a rival crew.

The man had been pushing for trouble and Sam Harper became the butt of the man's attack. Words turned ugly. The drover became dogged in his insistent torment-ing of the younger man. The more Harper tried to talk the mood down, the worse the drover became. And when the town's lawman tried to step in and calm the man the drover turned on him, laying a bottle across the man's skull and putting him down. An instant later he pulled his gun and started firing at Harper. A bullet tear in his arm forced Harper to draw. He saw no reason to die simply to appease the raging bully pulling down on him. In the face of direct fire he drew his own gun and put a bullet into his tormentor, directly over the man's heart. The drover was dead by the time he hit the floor. It did little to ease Harpers conscience that he had fired out of pure self-defence, that the lawman later testified so and Harper walked from court a free man, with a reputation he didn't savour.

The tale was well told and it followed him wherever he went. The down side was that it brought others out of the shadows. Men who figured they had to go up against him in order to bolster their own egos. He tried to turn his back on them. That failed to stop the challenges and his gun came out on a number of occasions in order to keep him alive. Finally he broke away and lit out on his own, seeking the empty high country, where there were few if

116

any who might step up to brace him. He started in catching wild horses, taming them down and selling them to the army and traders. Still not twenty-five he was a mustanger with a nice little business.

He took up with a young woman he met down along the Wind River, the daughter of a rancher he did business with. It went fine for a year until an old flame stepped into the picture and won the girl back, leaving Harper with an empty feeling in his gut and a need to move out of the area. His need for company took him back to a town where he decided to settle for a time. It went well until someone recognized him and the would-be gunslingers started to show up. As before he tried to walk away. And, as before, it failed to work. He killed two men who refused to leave him be and then moved on. His name followed him.

A lawman in the Nations persuaded him to pin on a badge and use his gun skills to aid him in bringing in renegades and assorted bad men, and he did that for almost three years. It became his way in life. He stayed until his reputation added too much to his burden, then moved on again. He drifted, his skill with the gun and his solid work as a lawman always allowing him to pick and choose where he worked. He had a spell working as a scout for the army, held a few more jobs as a deputy in a number of towns, then drifted into the less high-profile profession of working for bounty. It left him to work on his own, within the law, but riding the edge. Being a lawman put others at risk when the glory seekers came to call and he refused to accept the responsibility. So he took to hunting men for the reward on their heads.

At the back of his mind lay the thought that if he

saved enough of his bounty money he might one day have enough to start his own place again. It was a dream, but at least it allowed him a goal to strive for, and it gave him a degree of contentment. For once he seemed to have found his way. The work was demanding, solitary, but he took to it and he might well have stayed with it if it hadn't been for the incident in San Felipe when he had braced the three men he had been following for almost two weeks. Harper had faced them, asked them to stand down and get rid of their guns. It was a request he had to make, knowing from past experience that it was seldom accepted as the only way out for a bunch of desperate men. The trio had sneered at his request and in the blink of an eye they were going for their guns. The confrontation was started and finished in seconds. Bullets flew, targets were found, and Harper's trio of living renegades became dead renegades. But not before one of them had got off two shots that hit home. One in his shoulder, the other glancing off his skull with sudden, stunning force. He barely had time to register he had been hit before everything went away in a blinding flash. And then darkness and the aftermath when Harper finally woke and had no idea where he was – and worse, *who* he was.

The flood of images, memories, were all competing for his attention. They jostled busily, crowding his brain and pain rose, threatening to burst his skull wide open. A final, searing burst flashed across his eyes. Harper fell back, gasping for breath, sweat beading his face.

What the hell was happening to him?

Why now? Here of all places? He tried to speak but no sound came from his throat. He lay helpless . . . drifting

118

. . . visions of his life rising before his sightless eyes, filling the void of night with phantom shapes. He tried to sort it into some semblance of order but failed, and though he didn't realize, through sheer exhaustion, he finally slept. . . .

Harper opened his eyes to the steel-grey light of early dawn. He lay still watching the snow which still fell from the bleak sky. He gradually became aware of his surroundings. He felt the Virginia's pleasant closeness, the enticing warmth from the melding of their bodies. Sometime during the night she had curved herself to fit tightly against him. Her head lay against his chest, one arm was drawn tightly round him and she had thrust one leg between his thighs. No doubt her actions had been brought about by a desire for warmth and security during the long night. It made little difference. The result was just as disturbing as it would have been if she had done it through passion. And right at that particular moment Harper found he was ready to accept whatever it brought. He drew comfort from her intimate closeness, the soft woman scent of her, the caress of her hair on his unshaven cheek. It had been a long time, he realized, since he had experienced such a sensation and it drew him back to a more familiar world.

He had already realized something else: after the tumult of the night before his memory had returned. There were no more blank spots, no dark sections lurking in the recesses of his mind. He remembered everything. Of who he was, of where he had been and what he had done. Beside him the sleeping woman murmured unintelligible words. Her warm breath touched his cheek. Her eyes opened and she stared at him for long seconds, her sleep-drugged mind slow to react. She lay still, letting the thoughts gather themselves and when she had, a gentle smile curved her soft lips.

'Is everything all right?' she asked then.

Harper nodded. He was suddenly reluctant to move, to break the seductive warmth created by their entwined bodies. He reached across and brushed a stray lock of dark hair from Virginia's pale face. She smiled at him, almost shyly, but she made no attempt to disentangle herself from his body.

'You slept well,' he said.

'Lord, I've never been so tired.' She studied him intently for a while. 'You need a shave.' Her finger emerged from the blanket and traced a line along the taut line of his jaw.

'Yes, ma'am,' Harper said, and a rebellious thought rose in his mind. He acted on it, as he always acted on his instincts, and kissed her. Virginia's soft mouth parted, moistly warm. She rocked gently against him, gripping him tightly with her arms. Letting her supple body do her talking for her, silently enjoying the gentle exploration of his hands as they moved about her. It was a long time before their lips separated.

'It's surprising what a few hours' sleep can do for a man,' she said breathlessly.

Harper only smiled. He bent his head and kissed her again. He could feel the thrusting way her lithe body curved against his, the urgent pressure of her hips, the lift of her legs.

'Sam . . .' Her tone was heated, needful.

That was when Harper heard the sharp crack of a snapping twig. It was unmistakable. A brittle sound in the early

120

morning silence, it was hard to pinpoint from which direction, or just how far off.

What mattered was the fact that they were no longer alone!

13

Cole Shannuck stared at the broken twig beneath Jerome Cortland's boot and his eyes shone with rising fury.

'Why don't you just yell out we're comin',' he snapped.

'You don't intend telling me he could hear that?' Cortland retorted.

'Sound like that carries a long way up here. Jesus, mister, this ain't New York. Out here a man's life can he thrown away because of something like that. Remember one thing: Harper's no ordinary gunslinger. He's hard and he's good. Damned good. That's why he's still alive. You believe it, Cortland, because if you don't he'll take you and you won't even know it happened.'

Cortland scowled at Shannuck's broad back as the gunman stalked on through the snow. If it hadn't been for the money involved, Cortland might have said to hell with it and quit. But he knew he couldn't do that. Now that Virginia Maitland knew he was behind the whole scheme he had to go through with it. She had to die, along with the man called Harper. If either of them got through to the law and told their story he was finished. Though he would never have admitted it to anyone, Cortland was starting to get scared. The whole thing was getting out of hand. *It was like a damn snowball,* he thought. It starts off small but if it runs away from you it gets bigger and bigger, until it's too large to control. That was the way the situation was developing. It had to be resolved out here in this lonely, desolate part of the country. Once that had been achieved he would be able to put the second part of his scheme into operation. That was more Cortland's style. Dealing with money, handling the financial side. He had it all planned out, right down to the last detail. He began to get excited again as he thought about the money. *All that money.* The millions he would be able to accumulate. And it could be done. He knew it could. It had to work. He'd put in too much time already.

He just had to. . . .

'Damn it, Cortland, get over here,' Shannuck's harsh tone demanded.

Cortland joined the gunman. 'What is it?'

Shannuck lifted an arm, pointing with a gloved finger. 'There,' he said triumphantly.

A shout of excitement almost burst from Cortland's throat as he recognized the figures of Harper and Virginia. They were leading a horse out of the tangled cover of some thick brush.

'Let's get them,' Cortland said eagerly.

'Wait, you damn fool,' Shannuck said, but he was too late.

Cortland had already stepped out of the shadows thrown by the trees, lifting his rifle.

'Goddamn it, Cortland, don't,' Shannuck began. His words were drowned in the crash of the shot from Cortland's rifle. The sound rattled back and forth across the white snow. And Cortland was running forward, levering his rifle for a second shot.

The distant figure of Harper twisted toward the sound of the shot. His own rifle moved, fired. The distant report of sound was flat and faded quickly. Shannuck saw Cortland stumble, fall face down in the snow. Shannuck cursed wildly. He threw a couple of shots in Harper's direction, knowing he was way off, and angry at his own stupidity, he lunged forward through the falling snow to where Cortland lay unmoving. He bent over Cortland, savagely hoping that the man was dead. His hope was dashed when Cortland moved, a low groan coming from him. He lifted his head and stared at Shannuck.

'Did you get him?' he asked.

Shannuck stood up, staring into the distance. 'You scared him off. Christ, I seen some stupid moves, but you ought to get a medal, Cortland!'

Cortland struggled to his feet. 'Don't forget who's paying your wages on this job, Shannuck. If I hadn't lost my footing I might have got Harper.'

Shannuck laughed softly. 'Cortland, if he'd been bending over right in front of you I don't reckon you could have put a bullet up his ass!'

'Damn you, Shannuck. . . !'

'What in hell is going on?'

Shannuck glanced toward the speaker. It was Ben Holland. Close behind him was Cooper. Following was Holland's remaining bodyguard, leading the horses.

'*Well?*' Holland demanded. He stared between Cortland and Shannuck.

'Ask this damn New York gunfighter,' Shannuck said. 'I had Harper spotted. A good chance. Then he starts in like he's General Custer and balls the whole thing up!'

124

Ben Holland sighed wearily. He was cold, wet and hungry. He had spent a miserable night out on this damned mountain, trying to keep warm while it snowed on him. He was sick of the whole affair and if there had been a way out he would have taken it willingly. He was, though, in it right up to his neck. There wasn't going to be an *easy* way out. He had committed time and money and men. He just wanted to get it settled, take his share of the spoils and move on. Jerome Cortland wasn't making it any easier and it was unfortunate he had decided to come out from New York and take personal charge. The other unfortunate reality was that without Cortland the whole scheme couldn't be completed. If Cortland died everything was lost.

'Cole, why don't you and Cooper ride on ahead. Handle it your way. Just make sure Harper and the girl don't get to Bannock, or speak to anyone. We'll follow on. If you need us let us know. Safer if we wait at the other end in case you need backup in town.'

Shannuck glanced across at Jerome Cortland. The man had a fixed, bitter expression on his face but he said nothing.

'Sounds fine to me,' Shannuck said. 'Mr Cortland?'

Cortland saw it as a way he could bow out with at least some dignity. 'We'll do that. Makes sense to expand our options.'

'Jed, bring the horses,' Shannuck said. 'Let's just hope we can reach him fast. It ain't all that far to Bannock now.'

Cooper brought the horses. They mounted up and rode off. Holland watched until they had vanished in the misty snowfall. He hunched his shoulders beneath his thick coat.

'If there's a chance Shannuck will pull it off, Jerry,' he said. 'Let him do the dirty work. It's what you're paying him for.'

Cortland didn't answer at first. He seemed lost in thought. After a time he glanced at Holland and said, 'It wasn't right, you know, Ben, leaving all that money to a woman! It just wasn't fair!'

Holland glanced at his bodyguard. He was getting sick of hearing about how bad the world had treated Jerome Cortland. But he kept his mouth shut, even though he was fast realizing that he'd been a damn fool to let Cortland talk him into the deal in the first place. Snatching up the reins of his horse, Holland swung into the saddle and turned the animal in the direction of Bannock, his man close by and Cortland bringing up the rear.

14

Harper didn't hear the shot but he felt the horse shudder as the bullet struck. The animal floundered in the deep snow. It left a trail of red behind it. Harper knew it wasn't going much further. He freed his feet from the stirrups and slid from the saddle, dragging Virginia with him. They sprawled face down in the icy snow, struggling to make their feet

'Keep your head down,' Harper snapped at Virginia. He stared over her shoulder, his eyes searching the snowy mist.

Damn! Where were the bastards? He blinked his aching eyes, sore from the ever-present glare of the white carpet of snow. Then he spotted a grey shadow, a man on a horse, drifting like some silent ghost from the cover of tall pines. So where was the other one? Two had been following them for the past couple of hours, always at a distance, but closing persistently.

'Sam?'

'Wait,' he said.

She made to speak then thought better of it.

Ah! Now he saw the second rider. Closer, this one. Moving slowly. That would be Shannuck. He *had* remembered the man now. He knew of the man's past reputation. A tough son of a bitch, Cole Shannuck. Not a man to be taken lightly. He'd sooner kill a man than waste time on words. Harper squeezed Virginia's shoulder.

'When I tell you, get up and run! To the left there. Into those rocks. See them?'

'Yes.'

Virginia's tone was subdued. He knew she must be terrified.

'We'll make it,' he told her, trying to sound convincing. He cocked the rifle, took a deep breath, and rolled over. Jerking upright he aimed the rifle at Shannuck's horse and pulled the trigger. His bullet kicked up snow feet from the animal. It sat back on its hindquarters. Harper swore and aimed again. He pulled the trigger. The rifle slammed against his shoulder in recoil. Shannuck's horse gave a shrill scream, stumbled, went down and Shannuck spilled from the saddle hard.

'*Now*,' Harper yelled. 'Just run!'

He sensed Virginia acting on his instructions. There was no time to see how she was. Shannuck's partner was driving his horse forward, white spumes of snow rising into the air. Harper shot a quick glance in Shannuck's direction, saw that the man was still down, dazed, crawling around on his hands and knees. Shannuck's partner was yelling wildly at his horse, urging it up the slight rise of ground directly below Harper. The animal struggled as it ploughed through the deep snow. The rider had his rifle up and he began firing, trying to stay upright in his saddle. Bullets whacked into the ground around Harper. Dropping to a crouch Harper shouldered his own rifle and returned fire.

He missed altogether with his first shot. Then he steadied himself, ignoring the tug of a bullet going through his thick coat. His finger eased back on the trigger. The oncoming horseman went back out of the saddle like an acrobat. He slid off the horse's rump and landed face down, as if he'd done a belly-dive into a pool of water. There was a moment's confusion as the man's horse hesitated. It kicked up a mist of snow before it half turned and trotted off unconcerned. As the snow settled, Harper saw that the shot man was on his feet. Blood stained the front of his coat, pulsing out of the ragged hole. The man had lost his rifle. He tore open his coat and dragged out a handgun. With startling suddenness he began to fire, stumbling through the snow towards Harper. He was badly wounded but still capable of killing. Harper stood his ground. He lifted his rifle reluctantly and put three quick bullets into the man, determined to put him down for good. Shannuck's partner spun violently, his body ripped open by the shots. His gun hand jerked wildly off to one side, triggering a last shot into the grey sky. Blood sprayed across the snow, red then pink. The man lay on his back, twisted in the ugly sprawl of death.

Harper searched for Cole Shannuck. The gunman's horse was still there but Shannuck had gone. Harper picked up a line of tracks cutting across the snowy ground. Shannuck had broken for the same line of rocks Virginia had been making for. Harper swore. He turned and ran for the rocks, following Virginia's footprints. He slipped in the snow and almost fell. Sweat was cold on his flesh under his shirt. Only now could he feel the stinging pain of a bullet crease across his side. He recalled the bullet tugging his coat.

He reached the jagged line of rocks, plunged in amongst them unheeding. Something made him stop. He listened. Only silence. He crouched beside a slab of rock, reloading the rifle.

'*Virginia?*' he yelled.

There was no reply. Harper shoved away from the rock and moved forward. A gunshot split the air. The bullet whacked the rock close by, vicious splinters burning the side of his face like a thousand tiny needles. Harper threw himself to the ground, rolling frantically across the hard earth. He banged up against the closest large rock and crawled into its cover. He listened, ears straining for any slight sound. He knew, though, that Cole Shannuck wasn't going to be giving anything away. Harper would only hear what Shannuck wanted him to. *Well*, he thought, *sitting here isn't going to do any damn good!* He came to his feet in a lunging run, making for the cover of some taller rocks. He had almost reached them when the blast of shots reached him. Something burned across the top of his left shoulder. Bullets gouged white marks in the face of the rocks just ahead. Harper twisted to the left, making a desperate leap for cover. He hit the hard ground with enough force to make him gasp. Kicking himself forward he thrust his body into a narrow gap between two high boulders. Sharp stones tore at the flesh of his hands, snagged his clothing, and he left behind a trail of bloody fingerprints. Behind him he heard a rattle of falling stones. Hard boots clattered across loose shale.

Shannuck.

Turning about Harper sat up, peering around. A slither of sound came from his right. He spun round, caught a fleeting glimpse of Shannuck's powerful figure as the man

130

ducked around the edge of a thick boulder. Harper shoved to his feet, jerking the rifle to his hip. Up ahead, in the jumble of rock, Shannuck appeared. He was casting about urgently. He lifted his head and saw Harper.

'*This time, you son of a bitch!*' Shannuck roared. His rifle swept up and he snapped off a shot.

Harper had moved the moment he set eyes on Cole Shannuck. He was already in motion as Shannuck fired and the bullet missed. Then Harper's weapon blasted, the sound of the shot echoing in the confines of the rocky enclosure. Shannuck fell back as Harper's bullet caught his left hip. He slithered along a section of slanting rook, cursing the pain in his hip.

'Shannuck. You ready to quit?' Harper yelled.

Cole Shannuck's voice boomed out, 'The hell with you, Harper. Just show yourself and you'll see if I'm quitting.' He fired a wild shot in Harper's general direction. 'Come on, show yourself! I got money riding on your hide! Let's see you! I'm going to shoot your *cojones* off, Harper, you son of a bitch!'

Harper had circled the boulder he had used as cover. Now he found he was able to approach Shannuck from the man's right. Harper flattened himself against the boulder. He propped his rifle against the rock and took out his handgun.

'Shannuck, just stand easy! I've got a gun on you so. . . .'

Cole Shannuck swung round, his rifle lining up on Harper. They fired in the same split second of time. Shannuck had a wide grin on his face. It was still there when Harper's bullet tore open his throat in a burst of red. Shannuck slid across the slanting rock, still attempting to use his rifle. There was an animal urge in the man to keep on fighting. He braced himself against the rock, using the rifle one-handed. Incredibly he seemed oblivious to the blood pouring from the gaping wound in his throat, though he was coughing horribly. Before Shannuck could fire again, Harper's Colt winked flame a second time. The bullet drove into Shannuck's skull, smashing his head back against the hard rock. Shannuck hung against the rock for a time until his legs gave and he slithered to the ground in a welter of blood. The rifle slipped from nerveless fingers and Shannuck toppled face down in the snow.

Harper walked slowly across to where Shannuck lay. He punched out the empty cases from his Colt and reloaded. He didn't bother to check if Shannuck was dead. He didn't really give a damn. But he still kicked the man's weapon clear.

'Virginia? It's Sam! You can come out now.'

He turned as he caught the sound of disturbed stones. Virginia came out slowly from behind some high rocks. She held her revolver in her right hand, the muzzle hanging down. She looked stunned, lost, her face pale and sick. As she approached Harper she averted her eyes from Cole Shannuck's bloody body.

'There's a loose horse out there somewhere,' he told her. 'Let's see if we can catch it. Be a damn sight better than walking to Bannock.'

'What about the others?' Virginia Asked.

'I haven't forgotten them and you can bet they ain't forgotten us. So the sooner we move the better.' He recovered his rifle. 'Let's move.'

The horse was standing out in the open. Harper left Virginia under cover and walked out to where the animal waited. It lowered its head as he approached through the falling snow. For a few moments Harper was sure it would move off. He spoke quietly and the horse stayed where it was. Taking the reins he led it back to where Virginia was waiting.

'Come on,' he said.

As soon as they were mounted Harper touched the horse's sides and they cut off across the open ground. A thick stand of trees lay before them. Guiding the horse through Harper brought it out on the far side and saw a long slope falling away before them.

'Is it far?' he heard Virginia ask.

'No,' he said, although he had no idea just how far off Bannock actually was. 'Just hang on.'

Harper noticed that the snowfall was easing off as they reached the base of the slope. He pushed the horse as fast as he dared, constantly scanning the surrounding snow-filled landscape for signs of Cortland and the other two. A nagging thought grew in his mind. If they knew the lay of the land it was possible they might reach Bannock first, wait for him there. Harper sighed. Made no difference which way he turned when there was only trouble on the horizon. He figured he was going to have to take the risk. He had to reach Bannock soon for Virginia's sake. She wasn't going to last forever being carted back and forth across the mountains.

Come to think of it, he decided, *he'd had enough of it himself.* Bannock was their destination. The kind of reception he received would just have to be tolerated. One thing Harper was certain of: it wouldn't be the red-carpet treatment.

15

Bannock was no showplace. It was a working town. It existed because of the mines and drew its life-blood from them. Bannock had no time for fancy frills. It was basic, rough, quieter than it had been in its youth, but still a hard, pulsing community. It clung to the rocky slopes of the mountain, its rutted streets slanting and steep. The mines themselves lay in the hills around it. The earth had been blasted and gouged and scarred as the toiling teams of men ripped the valuable copper from the heart of the mountain. Bannock served those men, supplied them, sustained them.

Today it slumbered beneath a thick shroud of white. The howling winds and the ceaseless snowfalls of the past weeks had gradually slowed the town's normal, frantic pace. The steep streets were almost deserted that cold day, close on noon, when Sam Harper and Virginia Maitland rode in. The snow had stopped falling hours back. Even so a strong, bitter wind had sprung up and sliced down off the bleak heights above Bannock. Turbulent eddies stirred white clouds of icy snow off rooftops, sending it hissing along the empty streets.

Hunched over in his saddle, Harper eased the plodding

horse to a halt. He stared at the town. His eyes roved back and forth. There were dozens of places for an ambush to be set up. He had no doubt now that Cortland and company would make their play here in Bannock. They had to. It was their last opportunity, and they would take it soon. A final, desperate stand.

He felt Virginia stir. Her head had been resting against his shoulder. Now she raised her head and looked about.

'Where are we?' she asked. 'Is this Bannock?'

Harper nodded. 'Where's the marshal's office?'

'The far side of town,' she said.

'With our luck it had to be.'

Virginia surveyed the silent, empty street stretching before them. 'Do you think they're here, Sam?'

'I'm damn certain of it.'

'Surely they aren't going to try anything here in town. I mean Jerome's plan was for me to have some kind of accident. Get lost in the snow out on the mountain. A natural death. Not have me shot down here in Bannock.'

'That was the original idea. But things have changed now. We know what was planned. We've seen faces. As long as we're alive we represent a threat. Cortland's plans might be fouled up, but if he can kill us he might still get away with his life. And if he can do it without being identified he could still salvage his scheme. I figure he's desperate enough to make a try.'

Virginia sighed. 'I'm sure you must regret having got mixed up with me.'

'And given up the chance of such a trip? Look what I'd have missed.'

'Sam Harper, you must be mad.'

'Yeah? I probably was at the time I signed on.'

135

'Oh? If you hadn't been ill maybe you would have said no.'

He turned in the saddle to look at her.

'Crazy or not, I wouldn't have turned *you* down.'

'Comforting thought. Why? Was it my persuasive powers?'

'That was one of the reasons I came along.'

'What was the other?'

'Not the place to discuss that.'

She gave him a ghost of a smile, one curved eyebrow lifting. He saw she had the modesty to blush slightly.

Harper surveyed the street for a second time. There was no point in just sitting where they were. A bullet could find them whether they were on the move or motionless. Harper opened his coat and made sure he could get at his Colt. Touching his heels to the horse's sides he moved it on, letting it choose its own pace.

Every window, every shadowed doorway posed a threat. Cortland and his partners could be concealed anywhere along the length of the street. Down any alley. On a rooftop. Maybe letting Harper ride by so they could step out and put a bullet in his back.

Or Virginia's.

Her safety worried him more than anything. On his own he could have coped with the minimum of concern, but he had her life in his hands. An unfortunate facet of his returned memory was the knowledge of others who had died because of him. There were too many. He didn't want it to happen again. Not to Virginia. Not now. Not since. . . .

'*Sam!*'

Virginia's screamed warning came a second before she

136

pushed him violently to one side. Harper felt something jolt the saddle beneath him. Seconds later the sound of the shot reached his ears. He kicked his feet from the stirrups, letting his body slide from the saddle. As he went down, he grabbed at Virginia's coat, pulling her with him. They hit the ground in a tangle, thick snow cushioning their fall. Harper caught hold of her arm, his other hand snatching the Colt from its holster. Half on his feet he threw a quick glance across the street.

Saw nothing. He raised his eyes to roof level and saw a dark figure skylined against the white background. Light rippled along a rifle barrel. Harper snapped off a hasty shot, knowing he'd not hit anything. But the shot threw off the other's aim. The return bullet which came seconds later was yards off target too.

'Up,' Harper yelled. He hauled Virginia to her feet, shoving her toward the closest building, trying to keep himself between her and the gun across the street.

As they stumbled up the boardwalk, more shots rang out. Now there was a second rifle. A window exploded above Harper' s head. Wood splinters blasted out from the frame of the door Harper was trying to open. It was locked. He smashed his shoulder against it. The door creaked but held. Bullets thudded into the wood around him, and Harper thought that it wasn't going to be long before that son of a bitch on the roof got his range, and that would be it. Cursing wildly he threw his whole weight against the door. Something cracked and the door flew open. Harper stumbled, regained his balance. He reached out and took hold of Virginia's sleeve. She uttered a stunned cry as he hauled her brutally in through the door, the force of his action throwing her to the floor where she lay in a daze. Stunned, she raised her head. She could feel blood running down one cheek from a cut. She looked around for Harper but he had gone out through the door in a loping run, moving sharply along the boardwalk, knowing he was doing just what they expected. He didn't give a damn. He was good and mad, to the point of recklessness, and though he knew he was going against the book, he was also aware of what he was doing. He heard the flat sound of the rifle again. The bullet whacked against the wall just behind him. Harper changed his direction, cutting in a deliberate line across the empty street. He caught sight of the man on the roof, standing to get a clear shot, and came to a dead stop. He lifted up the big Colt, double-fisted, aiming by pure instinct. He fired in the same instant as the other man. Something caught his left hip, spinning him round, and he went face down in the cold snow, a sick feeling swelling up inside. He twisted round, staring up towards the roof and saw the rifleman fall slowly forward off the edge. The man arced away from the building as he came down, curving almost gracefully. He began to scream. The sound was cut off abruptly as he hit the street, bouncing visibly, then lying still, face down.

Standing there, Harper could feel warm blood coursing down his side. There wasn't any pain yet, only a strange numbness. He was beginning to feel comfortable, a sensuous warmth spreading over him. He shook his head angrily, reminding himself there were two more of them somewhere. His fingers closed tightly around the wet butt of the Colt and he eased back the hammer. He waited.

Silence . . . then he heard the faint tread of boots crossing the crisp, frozen snow. Was it Cortland? Or had that been Cortland up on the roof? He somehow doubted it.

138

Very likely it had been one of the man's hired guns. The footsteps halted. In the sharp silence Harper heard the unmistakable sound of a gun being cocked and he knew he couldn't afford to wait any longer. He judged the man's distance, his position, and hoped to God he wasn't wrong.

And then he moved, curling his body round, thrusting out his gun hand, his eyes seeking his target. . . .

The man had his back to the sun and all Harper saw was a black shape. He heard the man's sharp intake of breath an instant before the clap of gunfire. Red flashes flickered from the muzzle of the man's unseen gun. Gouts of snow exploded around Harper's body. His own gun was slamming back against his palm, over and over until the hammer dropped with a solid click on spent cartridges. The dark figure seemed to leap away from Harper, twisting violently in a rictus of agony as the force of Harper's bullets slammed him to the ground where he lay kicking in a final spasm of pain.

Ignoring his own rising pain Harper pushed himself slowly into a sitting position, desperately trying to reload his gun. His left side was slick with blood. His fingers were thick, clumsy, refusing to respond. He became aware of figures emerging from the doorways along the street. He saw faces, curious, some indignant, others angry, and he searched among them for familiar features. He watched someone go to the man who had fallen from the roof, turn the body over. It was not Cortland. Harper climbed awkwardly to his feet, hugging his bloody side.

Damned if he wasn't tired of being shot just lately. How many times had he been hit during the last few days? Too many. He was out of condition. His responses slow.

139

He ignored the staring faces. He moved to stand over the second man. He recognized him as one of the men from the station. But not Jerome Cortland.

'Hey, that's Ben Holland,' someone in the gathering crowd said.

'Always said that feller would end up with his belly full of lead,' said another.

'What's been goin' on, mister?' A hard-faced man put his hand on Harper's shoulder. '*Just what . . .*' The man's tone dropped to a hushed whisper as he caught the full fury of Harper's savage expression and he took his hand away quickly, stepping back.

Harper shouldered the man aside. He had caught sight of Virginia coming across the street towards him, her face pale, eyes wide with alarm.

'Sam,' she called, and began to run.

Jesus, no!

Harper took a step toward her, feeling his legs weaken.

'Get back inside,' he yelled. 'Cortland's still around somewhere. For God's sake get off the street. . . .'

And then the street tilted. Everything went out of focus. He knew he should get Virginia back under cover. Cortland was on his own now, a desperate man. Maybe desperate enough to still try to get at Virginia. He plunged forward, wondering why Virginia seemed to be getting further and further away from him even though she was running in his direction. He was still trying to figure out the reason when the ground rushed up to meet him and the day exploded in a flash of brilliant light and mind-numbing pain . . . and then nothing.

140

16

The local doctor had dug the bullet out of Sam Harper's side three days back. Before that happened Harper had lost a fair amount of blood on Bannock's main street. He was unconscious for a day. When he finally woke up he felt weak but ravenous, and despite the doctor's objections he downed a good meal, refusing to have anything to do with the light diet of thin soup prescribed for him.

'You were terribly rude to him,' Virginia scolded, as she returned to Harper's hotel room after seeing the irate doctor out.

She closed the door with a bang and came to stand beside the bed, her beautiful face marred by a frown.

'He'll get over it,' Harper said. 'He's getting paid, isn't he?'

'That isn't the point, Sam. It's time you realized you just can't go through life being so bossy with everybody?'

'Yes, ma'am.'

'And don't treat me like a child.'

Harper studied her for a while. She had got rid of the bulky clothing she'd been wearing. Her hair was brushed and shining, falling to the shoulders of a snug-fitting

141

powder-blue dress. Apart from a few tell-tale bruises on her face she was looking incredibly lovely. There was nothing childlike about her.

'Where's the marshal got to?' he asked, trying to keep his tone pleasant.

'Mr Bailey will be along presently,' Virginia told him. She sat on the edge of the bed and stared down at him. 'How do you feel?'

'If you must know I ache all over.' Harper jabbed a finger at her. 'And I still want that meal.'

'Be patient, you grouch. I'm not surprised you're sore. The doctor said he was sure you ought to be dead. He'd never seen so many bruises and cuts on a man still walking about. Cracked ribs. Lacerations. A scalp wound. Bullet grazes. I told him you were just too stubborn to lie down and die.' Virginia's face softened and she reached out to touch his cheek. 'But I'm glad that's the way you are. And I am also glad you took time to have a shave.'

Harper put his arm around her waist, pulling her toward him. The scent of her perfume reached him.

'Want to help a sick man get better?' he asked.

A smile played about the corners of her mouth. 'How?' she asked.

Harper didn't say anything. He simply drew her down to him, letting his mouth find hers. Virginia responded warmly. His hand slid from her waist to the rounded curve of hip and thigh, fingers teasing the firm flesh through the clinging dress.

'Are you sure this is going to help you get better?' Virginia murmured.

'I'll let you know later,' Harper replied. In fact, a pleasing rise of anticipatory warmth was flooding his loins. His free hand explored the firm fullness of her upper body, moving with increasing pressure.

'Sam,' Virginia sighed, 'this is . . . is nice.'

Any response he might have made was destroyed by the sudden knock at the door. Virginia drew away from him, face flushed, hastily smoothing down her dress and rearranging her hair.

'This is getting to be a habit,' Harper grumbled sourly.

Her composure regained, Virginia crossed to the door and opened it. The man who stepped inside was tall and solid, his thick hair greying at the temples. He wore a dark suit, drawn tight across his powerful shoulders. A burnished badge was pinned to his dark vest. The well-worn gunbelt around his waist supported a long barrelled Colt with plain wood grips.

'Miss Maitland,' he acknowledged.

Virginia smiled. 'Do you have any news for us, Marshal Bailey?'

'No, ma'am.' Bailey glanced across the room to where Harper was watching him. 'Glad to see you're looking better, Harper.'

Harper knew the man from a few years back. Then Bailey had been working in Casper. Harper had visited the town to collect a prisoner for the local US marshal's office.

'I'd feel a lot better if I knew where Cortland was,' Harper said.

Bailey grunted softly. 'No more than I would. That feller has a lot to answer for. But he's just vanished. That's the plain of it, Harper. He just ain't to be found.'

'But where could he be?' Virginia asked. 'Jerome Cortland is a city dweller. He doesn't know a thing about

143

surviving in this kind of country. Especially in this kind of weather.'

'You'd be surprised the things a man can turn his hand to when the need arises,' Bailey said.

'Maybe he's made tracks for home,' Harper suggested. 'Jumped a train heading east.'

'A possibility,' Bailey agreed. 'Schedules are practically back to normal now the storms have blown themselves out.'

'Won't do him much good if he does go back to New York.' Harper said. 'Since Miss Maitland telegraphed her main office they've disassociated themselves from his law firm. Closed down his access to any accounts.'

'Every lawman between here and the east coast will be on the lookout for him,' Bailey affirmed. 'Bit of luck for us that none of the telegraph lines came down during the storms.' Bailey paused before asking, 'What are your plans now, Harper?'

'Finish this business one way or another.'

Bailey nodded. 'Yeah, well, I'd better get back to mine. I'll look in again. Keep you posted. But I figure by now this Cortland feller has either froze himself to death some-where or he's taken off. When we checked with New York and they told us he was supposed to be up in Canada on a hunting trip we followed it through. Seems that was the way he got here. But he ain't gone back. You ask me – I think he's running.'

After the marshal had gone, Virginia looked at Harper, her face serious. 'Do you have the same feeling as I do?'

'About Cortland?'

'Yes.'

'I only know one thing, Virginia,' Harper said.

'Cortland hasn't gone back to New York. He hasn't run either. He's still around. And I figure he's waiting his chance.'

'The sooner we leave the better.' Virginia returned to sit on the edge of the bed. 'The doctor said a couple of days at least. . . .'

Harper reached for her. 'The hell with him.'

'Maybe I ought to lock the door this time.'

Harper smiled. 'I think maybe you should.'

17

Two days later they took the first available train making the trip from Bannock to Butte. The doctor who had been treating Harper washed his hands of his irritable and ungrateful patient. He had decreed that a train journey was not advisable. Sam Harper decided that was nothing more than medical horseshit and he had said so.

He knew his own body better than any damn doctor. He was fully aware of what it could stand and, at that moment, the last thing he required was prolonged rest. He wanted – needed – activity. There was a longing inside him that demanded to be heeded and it said get the hell out of this damned place.

Now he sat across from Virginia, staring moodily out through the grimy, frosted carriage window, not really seeing the snow-covered mountain slopes, the silent, close-ranked pine forests. His mind was absorbed with other things, other places. He was thinking about picking up the threads of his old life. Wondering where they might lead him. To more danger? More violence? He already knew the answers. It was time he quit the bounty business. Chasing all over the country, putting his life on the line just so he could collect some hard cash. He knew he had a fair amount in a bank account. There was enough for him to kick off his horse ranch venture. That was something worth putting his sweat into. Time he stopped trying to run away from life and time he started living it. Taking everything into consideration there was bound to be a better way than his previous life. A brightness that would shine through the shadows. He glanced in Virginia's direction. She was definitely one of the brighter moments.

'Are they private?' Virginia's voice penetrated his sombre mood.

'What?'

She was smiling across at him. 'The thoughts,' she said. 'I wasn't sure I should disturb you.'

'Just thinking ahead,' Harper told her. He studied her for a moment.

She figured in his life now and there was no easy way around the fact. He wasn't sure he wanted a way round. He knew he wanted her in his life and even with everything she had going on for her, she had made it clear she felt the same.

'*Hey!*' Virginia leaned forward and prodded him. 'I'm still here, Sam Harper.'

'Trouble with getting your memory back is having to remember the way things really are. You and me together – it's just asking for trouble.'

'You explained it all very clearly last night,' she said. A faint flush of colour rose in her cheeks as she recalled the circumstances under which he had done his explaining. 'I think from now on I'll conduct all my serious conversations in bed. It adds a certain spice to the occasion, don't you think?'

Harper smiled. 'Miss Maitland, you're a shameless woman.'

'Am I? *Am I really?*' She eyed him provocatively. 'You should know.'

'Stop trying to change the subject. Listen, Virginia, I just don't want you to be hurt.'

'After what I've been through I don't think anything can ever hurt me again.' Virginia moved across to sit beside him. 'Sam, listen to me. You remember what I said last night? Your dream for your horse ranch? No reason we can't make it work. Forget my money. When I get back to New York I'm going to step down. Turn the running over to the board and let them handle the business.'

'You must be as crazy as I am.'

She smiled. 'Maybe. But I don't care. You asked me once if I wanted a home and a family. Remember what I said? Well, the right man has come along and that's all that matters.'

'Only on my terms,' he said. 'We do it on my money. No easy way.'

'But I could invest. Become a partner. On a strictly business level of course.'

'That only covers the ranch. Anything else is personal.'

'Mr Harper, I wouldn't have it any other way.'

When they reached Butte there were matters to be attended to. The train which would start them on their journey east wasn't due for a couple of hours. It gave them time to collect their belongings from the hotel where they had stayed before riding out for Bannock. They even had time for a meal before making their way down to the depot.

The train pulled in on time. Virginia had arranged for a private car to be reserved for them.

'Are you ready?' she asked Harper. Then was no reply. Virginia turned to glance at him. He was staring along the platform, a distant expression clouding his eyes. '*Sam?* Is something wrong?' She had been with him long enough now to be able to recognize the danger signs.

'I thought I . . .' he began, then shrugged the moment aside. 'Come on, let's get where it's a bit warmer.'

The train slid away from Butte in a cloud of steam and billows of thick smoke. The depot buildings quickly drifted from their sight. The empty landscape was a white nothingness of snow and cold, high peaks. Harper stared up at them, finding he had no regrets at leaving them behind. A lot of violence and death had been meted out up in those frozen mountains. He'd almost lost his life, yet had regained it too, in a way. Finding himself and finding Virginia were the only good things to have come out of the whole miserable episode.

'What's your timetable when we get to New York?' he asked, settling down in one of the compartment's comfortable seats.

'Business and more business,' she replied. 'Apart from the normal routine there is this Cortland affair to be sorted out. I have instructed that a new firm of lawyers be appointed to handle the legal side. Also accountants will have to be called in to sort out just exactly what Jerry Cortland managed to get up to and do what they can to reclaim what he stole. It's going to take time. I just hope

149

too many investors don't get hurt. So it appears I am going to be very busy for a time, Sam Harper.'

'I have a feeling you'll survive it all and come out still looking beautiful.'

She crossed the compartment and perched herself on his lap, arms slipping with familiar ease around his neck. 'And where will you be off to?'

Harper shrugged. 'First I make sure you're safe. After that I go hunting for a place to set up the ranch,' he said. 'Nothing's going to surprise me any more.'

'*Nothing?*' she murmured, playfully nibbling at his ear.

'We've got a long ride ahead of us, woman, so don't be so damned impatient.'

'I can't keep my hands off you,' Virginia whispered.

'So I keep noticing.'

'Well then . . .' Virginia began . . . but her words were cut off with sudden abruptness.

Harper had heard the soft click of the compartment door being opened. There had been the absence of a knock beforehand, ruling out one of the train's attendants. As far as Harper was concerned that meant only one thing: an uninvited intruder – and he knew just who – verifying that his instinct had been right back there on the platform of Butte's rail depot. He threw Virginia floorwards, rolling off the seat himself, grabbing for the Colt on his hip, feeling the stitches in his side tear and blood start to seep from the wound. As he hit the compartment floor he heard the solid blast of a shot. The bullet ripped its way through the seat, blasting leather and lining out in a wide fan. Harper twisted his body, jerking his head round so he was facing the door end of the compartment, pulling his Colt into line. A second shot filled the compartment with noise. Powdersmoke curled about in heavy coils. Harper heard the bullet chunk into the floor. He snapped up the Colt, triggering a swift shot in the direction of the dark figure lunging away from the door. He knew he'd missed the second he pulled the trigger. And then it was too late because the moving shape was on him, leaping towards him like some ravening wolf. Harper tried to bring his Colt up but there was no chance. The hurtling figure smashed into him, slamming him down against the floor of the compartment. Harper had a jarred impression of a wild, snarling face, eyes gleaming with some insane brilliance. The mouth was open in a grimace of pure rage, teeth gleaming white against the unshaven face.

Harper looked into that face, and saw that Jerome Cortland had slipped over the edge into madness. The man was wild, endowed with superhuman strength. He had thrown aside the gun he had carried and now he used both hands to clutch savagely at Harper's throat. Harper swung his gun hand up in a short, sharp arc, cracking the hard barrel against Cortland's skull. A pained howl burst from Cortland's lips. His hands left Harper's throat, fingers closing over the Colt's barrel, and he began to jerk the gun from Harper's hand. Harper drove his left fist against Cortland's side, over the ribs, again and again. Cortland lashed out with his right, delivering a brutal backhand blow to the side of Harper's face. The blow hurt, rocking Harper's head. Blood spurted from a split lip. The pain angered Harper. He put everything into a sudden surge, throwing Cortland from him. Yet Cortland still hung onto the barrel of Harper's Colt, dragging it from Harper's hand. Even as

Cortland was rolling away from him Harper stumbled to his feet.

He turned in towards Cortland as the man rose on his knees. Harper lashed out with his booted foot, catching the hand that clutched his own gun. The impact broke fingers and sent the gun flying across the compartment. Cortland howled at the pain of his fractured hand. He pushed to his feet and launched himself at Harper. Locked together they stumbled across the swaying floor as the train eased around a curve. The side of the compartment brought them to a stop. Harper gasped as he slammed against the compartment wall. He jammed a hand under Cortland's chin and pushed the man's head back, feeling Cortland grunting and straining as he fought back. They twisted and slid along the compartment wall. Harper pushed them away, feeling Cortland pulling back, then the man braced himself and summoned every ounce of strength in his body as he thrust back against Harper. There was a brief moment when nothing seemed to happen and then Harper felt himself off balance. He struck the compartment window at his back, heard glass break, felt the chill rush of cold air gust into the compartment. Cortland uttered a shrill cry of triumph, as if he had already won. Then his cry turned to a pained grunt as Harper sledged his right fist around and hit him across the jaw. The blow turned Cortland around, so his back was to the shattered window. Harper laid on his full weight, bending Cortland over the sill. Cortland felt himself being pushed through the window and uttered a scream of terror. One foot came off the floor. Cortland made a wild grab for Harper's jacket, dragging the man even closer.

Behind them Virginia called out as she sensed what was happening. She was too late.

The train leaned as it hit another curve and before she could make any kind of move the lurching coach tilted and Harper and Cortland were gone out through the window, vanishing from her sight.

There was no time to prepare for what happened. One minute Harper was struggling to overcome Jerome Cortland, the next he was in the air, turning over and over, the chill of the outside clawing at him as they fell.

Later he realized that if it hadn't been for the deep carpet of snow on the ground neither of them would have survived the impact.

Harper felt the cushioning layer absorb the fall. He sank deeply into the icy embrace of the thick snow. It enveloped him, got into his clothing and clogged his mouth and nose. For a time he lay stunned, coughing as he tried to clear his throat of the snow lodged there. He was on his back, staring up at the sky. His body ached from the fall, but there was nothing to suggest he had sustained any serious injury, though he could feel the warm flow of blood from the reopened wound in his hip. The doctor in Bannock would not have been impressed.

Cortland!

Where was Cortland?

Harper pushed himself into a sitting position, fighting his way out of the drift, and once he was on his feet he took a look around.

The train was way up the track, having come to a stop. Heavy smoke billowed from the stack, staining the pale sky. Distant figures were emerging from the coaches, staring in Harper's direction.

As he cleared the bank of snow Harper heard someone shouting from the direction of the train. He wasn't certain but it sounded very much like Virginia. If it was she was most likely berating him for doing such a reckless thing as falling from a moving train.

And in that instant he picked up a soft rush of sound and the sharp intake of breath. He turned in time to make out the blurred image of someone coming at him. It was Cortland. The man had got his hands on a solid snapped-off length of hard timber from a tree branch that had broken under the weight of snow. It was already cleaving the air as Cortland struck out. Harper was unable to prevent it from slamming against his body. The blow, wildly swung, had enough power to knock him off his feet. Harper fell back across the tracks, staring up at Cortland as he raised his makeshift club for another blow.

It would have been too easy to stay where he was, succumbing to the hurt and the threatening presence standing over him, but Harper still carried enough anger and a stubborn refusal to quit that enabled him to fight back. He struck out with the heel of one boot, catching Cortland dead centre on his right knee. The blow was delivered with a great deal of animosity, with intent to hurt, and it did. Cortland gave a scream as the hard heel impacted against his knee, fracturing the bone. His mis-timed swing slammed the club against the metal rail, splintering the wood. Harper rolled to one side, hauling his aching body upright, and turned back to face Cortland as the man lunged for him yet again. He moved awkwardly, favouring the leg Harper had injured and left himself wide open to Harper's hard-delivered right fist. It impacted against the side of Cortland's jaw, splitting the flesh and spinning Cortland aside. There was a brutal intent in Harper's actions as he struck again and again, his hard blows knocking Jerome Cortland back as each punch landed.

It was a savage payback for the misery and suffering Harper and Virginia had been put through because of Cortland's pure greed. A number of men were dead because of his desire to snatch away Virginia's wealth. The fact they had been working for Cortland, simply to fuel his desire for something out of his reach, made no difference to Harper. Cortland had lost any chance of forgiveness through his actions. Pursuing Virginia, forcing her to flee for her life, and placing her in peril took away the man's right to being forgiven. Man against man was acceptable. But any man who placed a woman in such a position rated low on Sam Harper's list. Pity had no place in Harper's thoughts as he hauled the man upright each time he fell, driving in blow after blow.

Cortland made his fight back, landing some telling blows of his own, tearing at Harper's face until it bled profusely. His retaliation only increased Harper's full-on attack and he gradually overcame Cortland's defence.

In the end they were reduced to a pair of battered and bloody creatures trading savage blows that inevitably could only have a single outcome.

It came as they struggled together, hands slippery with blood, the snow around them spotted pink. Harper landed a crippling punch that smashed in under Cortland's jaw, raising him on his toes before he stiffened and toppled over. He landed hard, the back of his neck crashing down against one of the rail tracks. Cortland uttered a short cry before he became still.

155

Completely exhausted, Harper, struggling to suck air into his burning lungs, sank his knees on the ground, head hanging, with blood dripping freely from his face. More blood glistened on his hip, where the torn open wound was still oozing. He supported himself on his splayed hands, knuckles raw and bleeding, and didn't even have the strength to look up when Virginia appeared, kneeling beside him. She gently raised his head, wincing at the fresh cuts and bruises on his face.

'God, you took awful.'

He managed a crooked smile. 'You always find the right word for every occasion. Must be that expensive English education.'

'Let's get you back on the train before you bleed all over the mountain.'

The conductor had accompanied Virginia. He went to look at Cortland and when he returned he was shaking his head.

'Mister, I don't know what it was between you two, but it's over now for good and all.'

'What do you mean?' Virginia asked.

'Yon feller isn't going to cause you any more trouble. Son, you got a powerful pair of fists there. He must have hit that rail pretty hard when you put him down. I figure his neck's broke. He's deader than yesterday's news.'

Harper climbed slowly to his feet, Virginia supporting him. The conductor, seeing the slick of blood spreading across Harper's side, added his arm and they all moved back to the train.

'Next stop I need to find the telegraph office,' Harper said. 'Let Bailey know about Cortland.'

'You the law, son?'

Harper glanced at the conductor. 'You mean you can't tell by my upright and clean-living demeanor?' Then he shook his head. 'Carried a badge a time or two. This time I'm kind of between jobs.'

The conductor glanced across at Virginia.

'He's been having a difficult day,' she said.

'That so, young lady? Then God help us all.'

Cortland's body was picked up and laid to rest in the baggage car at the rear of the train. Shortly it rolled on and the passengers settled down for the rest of the journey.

The conductor located an army surgeon in one of the coaches and the man did what he could for Harper, insisting he rested and didn't move until better medical help could be arranged. This man was no small-town doctor and brooked no nonsense. He made it clear Harper was not to make any kind of effort to get out of the bed in the compartment. The soldier, a ten-year veteran, who had served in New Mexico and Arizona, was well used to recalcitrant patients and threatened Harper with all kinds of hell if he disobeyed. He need not have bothered because Sam Harper had no resistance left in him. This time he had no intention of moving. He hurt, he was exhausted, and the kind of bedside manner Virginia was offering made it a distinct pleasure to be a patient.

When they were finally alone he lay and stared out of the window, watching her move quietly around the compartment.

'Hey, this isn't a wake for the dead,' he said. 'No need to tiptoe.'

She came and sat beside the bed, taking his bruised and raw hand in hers.

'I thought you were dead when you went out of that window.'

'Closest I ever been to flying like an angel.'

'I have a feeling you're too stubborn to die.' She leaned over to kiss his cheek. 'But I was still frightened.'

He watched her for a moment.

'He was off his head. Had to be the way he hid out just waiting his time. This was his last chance to make things right as far as he was concerned.'

'But it wouldn't have done him any good. The whole world knew what he'd done. The game was over and he had lost.'

'Man gets a notion in his head so strong he can't see the real world any longer. You were in his way. If he killed you everything would be all right again. That was all he could figure.'

Virginia shook her head. 'Poor Jerome,' she said. 'What a waste. All that for what? For nothing. It was all such a waste.'

Harper struggled to keep his heavy eyes open.

'Not entirely,' he said. 'If he hadn't forced you to come to Montana we wouldn't have met up.'

She considered that for a while.

'You're right. In that case then at least there's one good thing to come out of it all.'

He didn't answer and when she glanced down she saw he had fallen into a deep, and for once, untroubled steep.

She left him. It was time, she decided, that Sam Harper was allowed the chance to get his life back on track. He'd been through enough of late and for what lay ahead for them both, he needed time to gather his thoughts and push the flickering shadows of the past far behind him. If she had anything to do with it, his future would allow him to step into the bright light of day. If nothing else it would allow him the chance to see where he was going. And no one could expect more than that.